"Aren't you having a good time?"

Even in the moonlight Drew saw the sadness in her eyes. But she was beautiful, her eyes large and luminous, her dress floating around her figure.

"It's just...I don't know," she sighed. "I guess it's just that time is slipping away." Cathryn shook her head, unable to go into detail.

"A class reunion is a time to get introspective, isn't it?" Drew asked. "A time to take stock and wonder if the past fifteen years have been spent wisely and well."

Cathryn wrapped her arms around herself, trying to ward off the cooling sea breeze. "I haven't had time to do that. I've been so very busy, working very hard..."

"So many verys," he said softly, closing the distance between them and reaching up to caress her cheek. "Let me add one. I'm very attracted to you."

ABOUT THE AUTHOR

Pamela Browning is a former newspaper columnist, reporter and feature writer who began writing fiction when her children were small. As a free-lancer, she has written stories and articles for local, regional and national publications. She has also written under the names Pam Ketter and Melanie Rowe. Pam makes her home in South Carolina with her husband, son and daughter.

Books by Pamela Browning

HARLEQUIN AMERICAN ROMANCE

101—CHERISHED BEGINNINGS
116—HANDYMAN SPECIAL
123—THROUGH EYES OF LOVE
131—INTERIOR DESIGNS

HARLEQUIN ROMANCE

2659—TOUCH OF GOLD

These books may be available at your local bookseller.

Don't miss any of our special offers. Write to us at the following address for information on our newest releases.

Harlequin Reader Service
P.O. Box 52040, Phoenix, AZ 85072-2040
Canadian address: P.O. Box 2800, Postal Station A,
5170 Yonge St., Willowdale, Ont. M2N 6J3

Interior
Designs
PAMELA BROWNING

Harlequin Books

TORONTO • NEW YORK • LONDON
AMSTERDAM • PARIS • SYDNEY • HAMBURG
STOCKHOLM • ATHENS • TOKYO • MILAN

Published December 1985

First printing October 1985

ISBN 0-373-16131-X

Printed in Canada

Chapter One

Afterward, Cathryn wouldn't remember what her reaction was when she first saw Drew Sedgwick gazing at her from behind a pillar, his figure half hidden in the gloom of the darkened department store. Cathryn had heard of him, of course. Who hadn't? Drew Sedgwick had, after all, inherited a hole-in-the-wall store on Clematis Street in West Palm Beach, and in the space of ten years he had expanded that tiny store into a chain of department stores with branches in every major South Florida city.

And she remembered him from those long-ago days at Gold Coast High School, where he'd made a name for himself as a state all-star halfback in football and as captain of the award-winning swim team. She didn't, however, connect the man he was now with the boy he had been, a boy she hadn't known very well in the first place. And she was definitely unprepared for his impact on her life.

It was ten o'clock at night and after closing time, the only period when Cathryn could work without interruption at Sedgwick Department Stores' Palm Beach Mall branch. She was bone-tired; tired of shoving around furniture, tired of draping recalcitrant wads of fabric so that they hung gracefully, tired of trying to gussy up a corner of Sedgwick's to look like something it most definitely was not—a fashionable Palm Beach interior-design boutique.

Nevertheless, it was she who wanted to embellish her displays with the finishing touches, even though she could have called upon a number of her associates and apprentices. Cathryn Mulqueen, ASID, interior designer, trusted no one but herself to breathe life into her works, and the new Design Boutique was definitely one of her most important creations.

"Okay, guys," she said, blowing a strand of naturally pale hair out of her eyes. The hair drooped again, but it didn't prevent her from noticing the man who stood in the shadow of a column. Hands in pockets, he watched as she tucked her errant tresses behind her ear.

Cathryn's two helpers, Jeb and Elijah, sank down on the sectional sofa they had just toted across the floor. They were tired, too, and Cathryn was mindful that they were due at classes at Palm Beach Junior College at eight in the morning.

"Does that mean we're finished?" asked Jeb hopefully.

"Sure," said Cathryn. She dug into her skirt pocket. "Here's a few dollars. Go buy yourselves a hamburger and a milk shake on the way home."

"Aw, you don't have to..." objected Elijah. Eighteen and new on the job, Elijah felt uneasy about accepting the perks that came with it.

"I want to," Cathryn said, firmly pressing the money into his hand. She smiled at them through a cloud of fatigue. "Anyway, a well-fed employee is a satisfied employee. Now run along. And don't forget to show up at my studio after school tomorrow. I've got a few deliveries for you to make."

"We'll be there," said Jeb, hustling Elijah away. She watched as their faded blue denims disappeared rather eerily into the Linens section. Their Nike running shoes made no sound on the polished terrazzo floor.

In the cavernous silence of the empty store, Cathryn slowly massaged her aching back as she paused to take stock of the artfully arranged wicker furniture and bright pillows of flowered chintz. The three of them had done a good job setting this up. It would be ready for the customers when they flocked into Sedgwick's showrooms tomorrow in response to the newspaper ad campaign.

"That looks nice," said a deep voice from the shadows, and Cathryn jumped. She had forgotten all about Drew Sedgwick watching from behind the column.

Languidly he moved from the darkness of the obscure post and strolled toward her, into the light. The navy-blue of his classic Brooks Brothers suit looked almost black; his fine cotton shirt was white against his tan.

"You remember me, don't you? Drew Sedgwick. We graduated in the same class in high school. I admire your work."

Blue eyes sparkled at her; the hand he offered had nice fingernails, neatly clipped and squarish. Vaguely Cathryn remembered Drew and his high-school successes—wasn't it sports he'd excelled at? She'd hung out with the artsy-craftsy group. In any case, they'd inhabited different worlds.

Nevertheless, she attempted a smile. Her lips strained at the edges. Really, she was so tired. She hadn't expected to work this late.

He said, "Do you have time to take me on a tour?" And then, surprising her, he added a humble "Please."

Despite her exhaustion, Cathryn was unaccountably impressed by something behind the blue eyes. A kind of desperation or loneliness or longing. An innocence, too, and, so help her, a goodness. That was a lot to read into one look into a man's eyes, and it stopped her cold. *Drew Sedgwick*, she thought to herself in surprise. *I don't remember your being vulnerable in high school.* His self-assurance was still there; but in the old days he'd been too macho, a jock with a swagger. He was different now.

"It's almost midnight" she said, glancing at her watch to verify it. Deep shadows loomed in the nearby China and Linens departments; they were isolated here from the rest of the world.

"Ah," he said. She didn't know if that meant he would understand if she didn't conduct a tour, or if he was merely achnowledging the time.

"You can see what I've done," she said finally, deciding that he wasn't going to go away. He watched her, his lips parted, the light in his eyes warm and friendly. It confused her, this friendliness. Surely it wasn't predicated on their acquaintance so many years ago? Most of her memories of him were fuzzy, unclear. But the present reality of him was, well...so *real,* not fuzzy and unclear at all.

He gazed at her, blue eyes electric in their intensity. To hide her confusion she said rapidly, "I've placed just a few furniture items out here near the aisle to draw people into the Design Boutique. This is a wicker sectional, very unusual, imported from India." She went on in this vein, watching him, gauging his reactions to how she had decorated her assigned nook in his store. For some reason she needed Drew Sedgwick's approval for what she had done.

Cathryn still didn't know what had prompted the call two months ago from Sedgwick Department Stores' general manager. She'd been sitting at her desk, reviewing her accounts, in her paneled office hidden away in the patio atmosphere of her studio on the peaceful Via Parigi, off Palm Beach's exclusive Worth Avenue, when she'd answered the phone. Sedgwick's wanted to experiment with a new concept, the general manager had said. Bringing the skills of an exclusive Palm Beach interior designer to the discriminating customers at its mall store could change the store's image. Would Cathryn Mulqueen be interested?

Would Cathryn Mulqueen be interested? She didn't have to think twice. Cathryn Mulqueen was interested in anything that would bring her name before more of the public, anything that would stimulate business for her burgeoning interior-design studio, which she had built from the ground up.

Cathryn and the management of Sedgwick's struck an agreement, and her niche in Sedgwick's, to be known as Cathryn Mulqueen's Design Boutique, would open tomorrow. She wouldn't have to relinquish her thriving Palm Beach studio—far from it. The Design Boutique would be merely an adjunct to Cathryn Mulqueen Interiors. But the boutique would stimulate furniture sales for the store and publicize Cathryn's services to Palm Beach Mall customers. After all, Cathryn Mulqueen Interiors could make their homes more comfortable, more livable and more beautiful. Florida living, so casual and free, was an acquired taste for retirees accustomed to the faster-paced Northern style. And Cathryn, a graduate of Parsons School of Design in New York, was eager to help Northerners acquire that taste.

As Cathryn flipped quickly through her wallpaper sample books, she watched Drew from the corner of her eye. He had an exotic face—broad, bronzed and very regal. If she were designing a home for him, she'd include a few Egyptian accents—a big brass gong, framed hieroglyphics on papyrus matted in terra-cotta silk. His eyes were startlingly blue, so blue that she, who was used to tossing around the names of colors the way other people rattle off the names of their children, couldn't think of a shade to describe them. His hair was dark and styled with just enough carelessness to keep him from looking like someone who had stepped off the page of a magazine.

"I've had new business cards printed," Cathryn said, bending over the *escritoire* that would serve as a desk for the salespeople. She fumbled in a drawer for one of the distinctively embossed ecru cards, mindful that her naturally platinum-blond hair, worn loose and long, had fallen over her face. Before she straightened up, Drew's hand, almost of its own accord, reached out and brushed a single shining strand away from her cheek. His touch startled her so that she jerked away involuntarily and dropped the cards. They fanned across the thick fawn carpet at their feet.

Unnerved, she stammered, "L-Look what I've done."

"It's all right," Drew assured her quickly. "Anyway, it's my fault." He bent swiftly and with the grace of a natural athlete, scooped up the cards.

Something in his tone of voice, coupled with the reverent way he'd touched her hair, made Cathryn wary. The world was full of crazy people, and perhaps he was one of them. High school classmate or no high school classmate, she didn't know much about him.

"Really, I'd better go," she said, her usually low voice sounding unnaturally high, even to her. She swiveled her head toward the aisle, looking for the night watchman. She had seen him walking his rounds twice already tonight; surely he was still there.

"Please don't leave yet," Drew said, and a tone of dismay crept into his voice. "I was going to ask you to have a nightcap with me."

"It's much too late," she said, caught off guard. She pulled herself up to her full height of five feet eight and slipped her arms into her lightweight jacket.

"Well, perhaps. But you certainly can't go until you've straightened out that jacket. You've got it on inside out or upside down, and unless you're Houdini, you're not going to get out of it without help."

She shot him a quick glance; he was trying to suppress a smile. His eyes sparkled with devilment, and blue eyes weren't supposed to sparkle with devilment. They were supposed to remain serene, like the sky in summer, or, when angry, stab into you with cold fury like shards of ice. But these were indeed devilish eyes, fringed with black lashes intriguingly spiked together. Drew's smile was growing perceptibly wider.

The flush crept upward from her neck and spread across her cheeks. She hadn't blushed since she was a teenager. Thirty-three-year old women weren't supposed to react this way to men. She turned away to hide her flaming cheeks and fumbled with the front of the jacket, only to find out that he was right—somehow she had tangled the arms and twisted the back of the jacket in her hurry to get away, and short of contortions, she wasn't going to be able to set it to rights.

"Let me help you," he said, edging around the table. His face was only slightly above hers; he wasn't as tall as she had thought.

"I can manage," she assured him, her backbone becoming rigid. Her body seemed captured by confusion, and the touch of his gentle fingers on her neck didn't help matters.

"The only thing to do," he said patiently, "is to take it off." He slipped the jacket off her shoulders, and unexpectedly his touch sent chills through her.

"There seems to be something wrong with the lining," he said, and she turned to find him tugging at the fabric in puzzlement. "Ah, here it is, one sleeve is inside out. Now, let's try it again." He held the jacket for her, shaking it out a little, and smiled. There wasn't anything wrong with his manner, she decided. It was her own reaction to him that bothered her. That, and the bizarreness of this whole encounter....

She slid her arms through the sleeves, catching her hair beneath the collar. Before she could do anything about it, his hand slid under the weighty flaxen mass and slowly pulled it up and out until it unfurled, gleaming, across her shoulders.

"You have the prettiest hair," he said, almost as if to himself. "I remember it from high school."

Cathryn pivoted slowly to face him. "We barely knew each other in high school," she pointed out.

"I remember you very well," he said, longing to tell her instead that he didn't mean to come on too strong, but he had to keep talking because he didn't want her to leave, not now, not when he was just getting things started. "You wore your hair braided, with bright yarn threaded through the braids."

"Oh," she said in a small voice. He *did* remember her if he remembered that. The yarn had been her trademark, the difference, or so she'd thought, that set her apart from the other girls with long, bouncy hair and laughing eyes. It had been an affectation, a hey-look-at-me, I'm-different sort of thing.

"They used to call you Cat," he said, fascinated by her eyes, which were an unusual shade of green blended with gold. "Do they still?"

"No," she said. He remembered the yarn in her hair and her nickname. What else did he remember about her? What did she remember about him?

"Now, how about that nightcap? he said hopefully. "I know an out-of-the-way place where we can hear a terrific jazz trio."

She gazed at him, uncertain, her interest piqued. Admittedly, she was attracted to him. Furthermore, he was handsome and charming and all the rest, and he was clearly making a play for her. But wasn't he married? Her eyes automatically focused on the third finger of his left hand. Immediately she saw a telltale white stripe below his knuckle, a ring line that hadn't yet tanned.

"Recently divorced," he said quickly, answering her unasked question. Cathryn flushed again, wishing she hadn't been so obvious. But his statement told her all she needed to know.

She deliberately assumed a look of indifference before taking a step away from him. "It's very late, and tomorrow is a working day. It was nice seeing you again, Drew,'' she said formally.

He knit his brow. What had gone wrong? He *was* divorced—didn't she believe him?

"I'd like to call you sometime," he said quickly. He'd thought he'd made some headway. But just as she was beginning to become real and warm and alive to him, she took on the quality of finely sculpted crystal—lovely, but very cold.

"I'm afraid that won't be possible," she said coolly.

His eyes penetrated her expression. She caught her breath as he trapped her gaze; it was a long moment before her eyes escaped his. Without a word she turned and walked swiftly away into the darkness of the empty store, her heels clicking on the shiny terrazzo floor, her bright hair chasing the shadows.

He stood watching her as she ran away, for there was no doubt in his mind that Cathryn was running. She was turning away and he didn't know why.

Cathryn too, knew she was fleeing. She had not run from a member of the opposite sex since she was in the third grade and a boy had tried to lift up her dress. Then, she hadn't known what she was running from; it was like a game. Now she knew what she was leaving behind and she also knew that with Drew Sedgwick it was no game.

Well, he thought, rocking back on his heels, *there was still the class reunion. Surely she would be there...wouldn't she?*

JUDY CARRUTHERS had been Cathryn's closest friend since they had both refused to eat the canned spinach in the Northway grammar school cafeteria. Their refusal had earned them the admiration of their classmates and an hour of after-school chores, and Cathryn and the auburn-haired, freckle-faced Judy had become fast friends as they scrubbed down the chalky blackboards. They remained friends, growing up in the same close-knit West Palm Beach neighborhood, where they were encouraged by both sets of parents to think of each other's homes as their own.

Cathryn had been awed by the comparative luxury of Judy's home. Judy's father was a well-to-do attorney; Cathryn's father was a poorly paid clerk in an automotive store. The house where Cathryn's family lived was a run-down white stucco, small and cramped. Cathryn vowed in those early years that she would live like Judy and her family when she grew up.

Susannah Fagan came on the scene later. She arrived in the middle of seventh grade and possessed an enviably curvy figure and long black hair. Susannah managed to wriggle her way into Cathryn and Judy's closed society by craftily offering them lessons in how to flirt. Serious-minded Cathryn and bouncy, bubbly Judy had found Susannah's offer impossible to resist, especially when they saw the results of Susannah's flirting with the eighth-grade boys. Somehow they had become friends, the three of them, despite the total failure of Susannah's lessons. Cathryn and Judy hadn't learned to flirt until much later. Susannah sadly admitted after her second divorce that it was just as well that the two of them had been such late bloomers. In the long run, all flirting had done for her, she admitted, was get her into trouble.

Their three-way friendship had survived through high school and college, Judy's subsequent marriage and motherhood, Susannah's spate of marriages and divorces, and the demands of Cathryn's career. Ron, Judy's husband, was like a big brother to Cathryn, and their eight-year-old daughter, Amanda, was Cathryn's goddaughter. Susannah, a resident of New York City and an inveterate jet-setter, breezed into town from time to time for whirlwind visits, the purpose of which was to bring the other two up-to-date on what was going on in her hectic personal life. Susannah, Judy, Ron and Amanda were the only true family Cathryn had, other than a few distant cousins who lived so far away that Cathryn's only connection with them was a yearly Christmas card.

"TONIGHT'S LIKE OLD TIMES AGAIN," declared Susannah happily in her breathy voice one night two weeks after Cathryn had declined to go out with Drew Sedgwick. "Just think, a slumber party! We haven't done this since high school." Susannah hugged a soft down pillow to her ample breasts.

"Since the night before graduation," agreed Cathryn. The three of them were lounging in pleasant dishabille around Judy's big living room, Ron having conveniently gone out of town to complete a business transaction. Whenever they got together, it was always instant intimacy, no matter how long they'd all been apart.

"Fifteen years," mused Judy, the most sentimental of the three. "Can you believe it's been fifteen years?"

"With three ex-husbands, yes," said Susannah dryly, tossing her dark hair back over her shoulders. Susannah was currently between marriages.

"What I want to know," said Cathryn, "is why we're having a class reunion after fifteen years. Shouldn't it be twenty?"

"Because we never got around to having a tenth," Judy reminded her. "We were all too busy having babies and things like that."

"*You* were busy having babies," pointed out Cathryn. "*I* was busy working."

"I was busy getting divorced from husband number two," said Susannah reminiscently.

"Good grief, Susannah. Are you assigning them numbers now?" asked Cathryn, looking askance at her friend. Of Susannah's three husbands, Cathryn could only remember the first, and that was because he'd been extremely handsome. But Susannah ought to be able to do better.

Susannah stuck her tongue out. "Recalling numbers is easier than trying to remember their names." She paused dramatically. "Ah, yes, I'll never forget dear Whatsisname," she said, breaking into a wave of giggles.

Cathryn chucked a pillow at her. Still, she was slightly shocked by Susannah's cavalier attitude.

"Anyway," said Judy, making peace by passing the pretzels, "I can't wait until the reunion. They say Elbert Stuckey is extremely good-looking, can you imagine? Remember how he looked in tenth grade? Like a balloon with hands and feet." Judy puffed her cheeks out with air, pantomiming the hapless Elbert.

"Oh, but to balance *him* out, there's Vicki Sherman. She was homecoming queen and now she weighs two hundred pounds."

"So will I if I don't stop eating that Parmesan-artichoke dip," said Cathryn, pushing the potato chips toward Judy. "How dare you serve it? You know my weakness."

"Your weakness isn't food, dear Cathryn. It's work. I haven't seen you in weeks. Neither has Amanda." She turned to Susannah. "Do you know that Cathryn almost never dates these days? She turns down everyone who calls and asks her out."

"Do tell," said Susannah, licking dip off one dainty finger. "Are there any I'd be interested in? If so, send them my way. I'll be here for a week or so after the reunion."

"It's an idea," admitted Cathryn. "I've been too busy setting up my boutique at the mall even to think about going out with anyone. Say, Susannah, would you be interested in Drew Sedgwick?"

Susannah wrinkled her forehead. "Sedgwick, Sedgwick. You mean the guy who built up that chain of stores?"

"He was in our high school class," reminded Judy. "He'll probably be at the reunion."

"He asked me out for a nightcap late one night when I was working at the store," said Cathryn. As soon as she mentioned this, she regretted it. Somehow, her encounter with Drew Sedgwick, she realized too late, wasn't the kind of meeting she wanted to hold up to the scrutiny of her friends, even friends she trusted as much as Susannah and Judy.

"Didn't you go?" chorused Judy and Susannah.

"No," she said, and quickly she related the twisted-jacket incident, emphasizing its humorous aspects. She didn't refer to her inward physical response to Drew's touch; that was another story altogether.

"If you'll recall," said Judy patiently, "I tried to arrange a meeting between the two of you a couple of months ago. Drew is one of the most eligible bachelors around. Ron knows him. They met at a chamber of commerce breakfast, and Ron thought he seemed lonely."

Cathryn wrinkled her brow. "I don't remember your mentioning him." A succession of totally unsuitable blind dates had long ago convinced her to ignore Judy's perennial attempts at matchmaking.

"If you're not interested..." began Susannah.

"Of course she's interested," insisted Judy.

"But I don't know him. And he's just been divorced, and..." Cathryn was aware that she was talking too fast, but she couldn't seem to help it.

Judy's short auburn curls bobbed around her face as she shook her head in exasperation. "Don't you remember the story? About Drew and his ex-wife? I know I must have told you."

"What story?" Cathryn asked blankly.

"Talma—that's his ex-wife's name—suddenly decided to pursue a career as an actress and went off to New York City, taking their six-year-old daughter with her. I heard that Drew was devastated."

Cathryn experienced a sudden, crushing sense of disillusionment that surprised her. It wasn't as though there had been any pretense. Drew had told her immediately that he was recently divorced. It was why she had made her exit so abruptly, running from him like a child. She'd been burned once too often, and she avoided newly divorced men whenever possible.

"That's too bad," she said, hoping that she was successfully hiding her disappointment. But if he was devastatd by the divorce, she wanted nothing to do with him. It would never do in this instance for Judy to get a line on her true feelings.

"Now, Cathryn," began Susannah, adopting what Cathryn recognized as her let's-stop-and-think-about-this tone of voice. "I know how you feel about men who are trying to get over past relationships, but maybe he's different. Anyway, who's left? By this time, all the eligibles have been married at least once. Maybe even to me." She giggled again.

"Susannah," said Cathryn patiently. "Let's face it. Most divorced men qualify as the walking wounded, and Drew's no exception."

"So nurse him," said Susannah matter-of-factly.

"That," said Cathryn, "is exactly the point. Let me tell you about Drew Sedgwick. He's like all men in his situation—he's been through the worst sort of emotional trauma and he's desperate for someone to expend valuable emotional energy on him. He wants someone who will pick him up, dust him off, and put him back together again. And afterward, he'll find someone else, a woman who won't remind him of this traumatic period of his life.''

"Drew could be an exception, you know," Judy replied.

Cathryn remembered the yearning in his eyes, and she recalled how strongly she had been moved by it. Past experiences with such men had made her cautious, however, and she didn't need a man with flighty emotions in her life, now or ever. What in the world would she have in common with a high-powered department-store executive anyway? What would they talk about? His problems? *That* she didn't need. Or want.

"I don't think so," she said. "Just forget I ever mentioned him, okay?"

"If you insist," said Judy reluctantly.

"Must you insist?" asked Susannah.

"I insist," replied Cathryn in her most convincing tone. "And now, what are you two wearing to the reunion?" She thought it was the perfect question to nudge the conversation off the subject of Drew Sedgwick.

But, oddly enough, the next day Cathryn couldn't remember for the life of her what either Judy or Susannah had said they were going to wear.

Chapter Two

"Cat Mulqueen! Is it you? You look the same! Exactly the same! Doesn't she, Judy?" Shrieking at them was Myra Dinwoody, former captain of the cheerleaders, her shrill voice undiminished by time. Fascinated, Cathryn couldn't pull her eyes away from Myra's hair, which when last seen had been a mousy brown but was now dyed red for the festive occasion of their class reunion.

Judy, recovering first, laughed. "It's go good to see you again, Myra! I'd like you to meet my husband, Ron," and she drew Ron, owlish in his horn-rimmed glasses, into the group.

The class reunion had been in full swing for a couple of hours. They'd chosen the posh Breakers Beach Club, an adjunct to the grand Breakers Hotel on the ocean in Palm Beach, for their bash, and the first hour had been the most frantic, with screams of delight, warm embraces and broad grins very much in evidence. Now they had finished eating dinner, and a band was setting up to play for dancing.

"Oh, no," said Susannah under her breath. "Donny Paddock is going to throw Chuck Giles into the pool! Let's get out of here, Cathryn. It's likely to be us next!"

But on their way to the safe haven of the ladies' room, Susannah was whisked off to the dance floor by one of her innumerable old beaux, which left Cathryn on her own. She ducked behind a potted palm and watched in amusement as Chuck Giles, recently bald, swam fully clothed in the spacious inside pool, inviting everyone to join him. No one did, but Cathryn suspected that it wouldn't be long before Donny Paddock, always a rowdy, tossed someone else in to keep Chuck company.

Cathryn was feeling restless, and despite the hundreds of her classmates present, she felt lonely. She had dutifully oohed and aahed over numerous pictures of other people's children and accepted graciously her classmates' admiration of her own accomplishments as set down in the reunion booklet passed out to everyone at the door.

But now that she was alone, away from the crowd, her emptiness was a silence inside her, as though she were a ceremonial drum that had been beaten too loudly and then left while the celebrants danced away, caught up in their own music. Oh, she was proud of her studio, proud that she had been one of the few to discern the new direction interior design would take in gracious Palm Beach when condominium mania— otherwise known as condomania—descended on the island. She'd sized up the market and she'd stepped in with her own ideas, ideas about space and light and motion that she had incorporated into her designs. Acclaim had come to her early in the game; she'd become *the* interior designer to *do* the new places, and before long the doyennes of Palm Beach society, usually haughty and scornful of newcomers, clamored for her services. Soon Cathryn was delighted to find herself formulating discriminating interiors for Mizner mansions as well as for condominium penthouses and beachfront cabanas.

And she'd done what she had set out to do with her life. She lived luxuriously now, beyond her wildest dreams in the days when she'd envied the way Judy's family lived. She lived luxuriously, but alone.

With all her work, there hadn't been time for even a serious relationship, much less a husband or children. She'd never really minded until tonight when the accordion parade of wallet pictures had touched a nerve she never even knew she had.

Unseen by the merrymakers inside, Cathryn slipped through an open sliding glass door leading out to a low seawall overlooking the ocean. Her emerald-green Mary McFadden dress, its full silk skirt folded in minute pleats and spangled with tiny golden beads at the hem, flared around her legs in the breeze. Below, on the other side of the seawall, waves overlapped on the sand in scalloped swirls, the dark water beyond veined with a scant moon's skimpy embroidery.

Too bad about the moon, thought Cathryn. It should be round and full, so bright that it would hurt to look at it. As if to make up for the lacking moon, the scent of the sea filled her nostrils, banishing the mingled odors of cigarette smoke and people. The sliver of moon curved into a cloud; the brisk sea breeze lifted Cathryn's hair and made her feel light-headed. It had been a mistake to drink so much wine with dinner, she thought. She didn't know how long she stood there, thinking, withdrawing into herself, far away from the beach club and its neighboring hotel across the seafront road. And then she saw him.

She'd briefly wondered about him earlier—no, that wasn't true. It had been more than briefly. But Drew Sedgwick had not been in evidence at this gathering of former classmates.

"I saw you come out here," he said easily, detaching himself from the seawall several feet away. "Aren't you having a good time?" Even in this inadequate light she detected the flicker in his eyes.

"I didn't know you were here tonight," she said before she thought.

"I didn't know you were looking," he shot back, and then grinned.

She was beautiful, her eyes large and luminous, the green in them emphasized by the emerald silk of that gorgeous dress floating around her slim figure. Tall as she was, Cathryn wasn't lanky; she had exquisitely delicate bone structure, and her softly contoured facial features were arranged around a perfectly sculpted nose. The gold of her lashes was soft against creamy-white skin.

But when he saw the embarrassment his remark caused her, he sobered. "I arrived late," he explained. And then he added gently, "Why did you come out here? Is anything wrong?"

"It's just…" she began wistfully, and then stopped, wondering how to explain the elusive emotion that had unwittingly projected itself into her thoughts. But she wanted to explain, wanted to share it with someone, wanted affirmation that what she was feeling was valid. "It's just that I felt time slipping away, I guess." She shook her head, unable to go into detail. Her hair shimmered with lambent light, making up for the absence of moonlight.

"I know," he said gently, thoughtfully. "A class reunion is a time to become introspective, isn't it? A time to take stock and wonder if the last fifteen years have been spent wisely and well."

She wrapped her arms around herself, trying to quell the prickling of the skin above her elbows that she always felt when she was particularly in tune with another human being. It didn't happen often, that prickling.

"Yes," she agreed. "That's it exactly. Everyone has children, it seems; bright, smiling faces to pull out of a wallet. I can't imagine having *people* to show off. All I have is a series of decorated rooms, houses made comfortable for my clients." She shrugged. She wasn't saying this very well. She couldn't imagine why she was opening up to this man she barely knew.

Drew leaned against the wall beside her, staring out over the breakers foaming and curling across the narrow spit of white sand below. The stiff breeze cooled their faces and feathered Drew's black hair across his forehead. The pale moonlight rendered his blue eyes dark as slate. In his expression, briefly, Cathryn saw the familiar look of a more youthful, less wistful man.

"Regrets?" he said, his long, sudden glance making her pulse leap in her veins.

Cathryn shook her head. A wayward strand of her long hair strayed across his face; gently he lifted it and regretfully let it go.

"I never had time for marriage or a family," she told him. "I worked very hard, took the little bit of money I inherited from my parents and invested it in my business, made the right contacts. I enjoy my work. In the beginning I tackled one day at a time, which seemed to be the right thing to do, and now all of a sudden it's been fifteen years since high school and I've never been married or had a child. I've designed interiors for everyone else, but I've neglected my own." Cathryn wasn't talking about the interior of the place where she lived—her apartment was decorated imaginatively and according to her own excellent taste. She was describing her interior life, and she knew that Drew would sense what she meant.

When she dared to look at him, Drew Sedgwick was regarding her with respect and something more. Understanding, of course, and she admitted to herself in that moment that somehow she had known she should expect no less from him. What's more, there was empathy in his expression, and life had taught Cathryn that such heartfelt empathy with another human being was rare.

"Let's go to the Alcazar Lounge and have a drink," Drew said unexpectedly, inclining his head toward the hotel across the seaside road. "We can talk quietly there. Please?" Again the humble request; again, it surprised her.

Lights winked on and off behind windows high above them; the twin towers of the hotel were softly spotlighted against the black velvet of the sky. Palm leaves rattled in the wind. Cathryn stared at him, wondering what was the substance inside this man. When she took on new clients, she listened carefully to their requests, looked closely at their life-styles, and then interpreted all of her information to design a home that encompassed the person, the space, the light. What were the dimensions of Drew Sedgwick's interior? How did he need space, where might she let in the light? What kind of home was he seeking?

"I'd like to go to the Alcazar Lounge with you," she said gravely, wondering it if was her own husky voice she heard or whether it belonged to someone else entirely, someone she didn't know at all.

He favored her with a jubilant smile and tucked her hand around his arm as they walked beneath the green-and-white striped awning of the entrance to the Breakers, as they traversed the pink-marble floor of the grand hotel. Their banquette in the elegant cocktail lounge overlooking the ocean was strewn with soft cushions, Turkish style, and Cathryn sank into them gratefully. Her common sense told her to be wary of this man who she was convinced could cause her much hurt, but her emotions had the upper hand now. She was curious about him. What's more, she felt comfortable with Drew smiling at her so pleasantly across the table, looking not at all threatening.

The waitress delivered their drinks, and the sweet, mellow sound of the vibraphone in the band drifted across the wide dance floor. Drew leaned closer so that they could talk over the sound of the music.

"Fill me in on the years in between high school and now," Drew coaxed. "Your biography in the reunion booklet tells me that you went to Florida State and after that to Parsons School of Design. What then?"

Cathryn shrugged, wondering how her history could possibly be of interest to Drew Sedgwick. "I worked in New York City for a while, felt cramped. The urban environment wasn't right for me—I needed sun and sky and space the way I remembered them from growing up here in West Palm Beach." She sipped her drink reflectively. "I accepted a well-paying job with a well-known firm in California, and just when I was really getting into it, my father died, and within months, so did my mother. I came home and saw what exciting new directions Palm Beach was taking, everything burgeoning, people flocking from the North to find a place in the sun, and suddenly I knew I'd come home for good."

"But how did you get started in your career?"

"I plunged right in. Started a business, worked out of a little warehouse near the railroad tracks in West Palm Beach, met some people who loved my work, eventually ended up in my studio on the Via Parigi in Palm Beach. Actually, I've made it sound too easy. It was damned hard, if you want to know the truth." She laughed, and he liked watching her sparkle. Even cold crystal sparkled if you beamed light on it in just the right way.

"There's something about your interiors," he told her, because he knew her work well. Whenever he went into a home in Palm Beach, he knew instantly if the interior was a Cathryn Mulqueen design. It was the same flair that had made her wear yarn woven through her braids in high school. Her personal offbeat style stood her in good stead in her career. Cathryn knew how to free space from the boxy confines of a room and how to use color so that it shaped space and light into new dimensions. "Your interiors, well, they're...well, they're fantastic," he said, unable to think of words that could adequately convey his enthusiasm for her work. "It's about time someone got rid of the heavy Spanish furniture that's been de rigueur in Palm Beach for too long, and you did it. You've also done away with all those thick wool rugs covering up perfectly beautiful tile floors, a fact for which I'm truly grateful. In fact, sometime I wish you'd design something for me."

She smiled. "Just drop by my boutique," she told him with a merry glint in her eyes. "It's at Sedgwick's at the Palm Beach Mall. They'll set up an appointment for you."

He laughed. "Is that all I have to do to get an appointment? I thought it would be more difficult, somehow."

Her smile faded. "Oh, Drew. You're very nice. But I'm very busy. I work very hard. I—"

"So many 'verys,'" he said softly, his hand closing over hers where it rested on the seat of the banquette. "Let me add one. I'm *very* attracted to you."

"This isn't the way it was supposed to go," she said shakily, withdrawing her hand and closing it around the stem of her glass, which felt chilly after the warmth of Drew's fingers. She took another fortifying sip of her drink, and then another. Maybe the alcohol would anesthetize her against his charms.

"Things don't always go the way they're supposed to go," he said thoughtfully. "I think that's one thing we've gleaned from this reunion. Myra wasn't supposed to dye her hair red. Elbert wasn't supposed to transform himself into Bert and end up being the best-looking guy in the class. Chuck wasn't supposed to go prematurely bald. You weren't supposed to become a dedicated career woman who won't even accept a date, and I wasn't supposed to—" But here, after inciting her interest, he stopped in mid-sentence and gazed out the window at the ocean. A freighter slipped across the invisible horizon, a line of lights suspended in black space.

"You weren't supposed to what?" she asked in spite of herself. Their reflections stared back at them from the window, and his revealed the brooding lines in his face.

"Do you want to know my story?" he said softly.

When she nodded mutely, pulling her eyes away from their reflections in the dark window, Drew said carefully, "I was married and had a child, and I worked very hard to build a secure future for the three of us. That's how I thought of all the time I put in, all the hours away from home; I was working for our future. Then my wife left and took my daughter, and my future went with them."

Something tightened in her chest, and inadvertently her eyes flashed to his hand curved around his glass. The ring finger, with its revealing white line, brought back memories she'd prefer to forget.

Terry Ballard's ring finger had sported such a line. Terry had surfaced in her life at a time when she was vulnerable; her parents were gone, her secure job in California left behind for her own business in Palm Beach. Terry was a landscape architect with a prominent firm, and Cathryn had hired him to work out a landscaping concept for a house with an atrium. She'd been lonely, unsure of herself, and open to new relationships. Terry was not only handsome but affable and interested in her work.

His wife, he'd confided, didn't understand him. Why did she fall for that old line? Because he hadn't said it quite that way, not at first anyhow. He was lonely, he'd told her, and his wife was busy with civic responsibilities. A month or so after he met Cathryn, he filed for divorce. She had scrupulously remained uninvolved until the divorce was final six weeks later.

And then they began meeting for lunch, for dinner, for late-night drinks. He rushed her with a passion that could only mean he loved her. He told her that often enough, after all.

And the boys, his darling little boys. Cathryn had liked them a lot. They had been three and five years old—round, chubby kids with pink cheeks and pudgy limbs. She'd fallen for them the way she'd fallen for Terry: hard.

She'd swallowed Terry Ballard's hook and gobbled up his fish story. She'd listened, sympathized and shored up Terry's precious ego. She had loved him.

And then Terry had called her three days after their last date to tell her he'd just married a woman he'd met at the jai alai fronton two weeks before. He'd acted hurt when Cathryn was too speechless to offer congratulations.

Cathryn had a hard time getting over Terry, but it had been just as hard to get over the boys. She still remembered the way Joey's quick smile had captured her heart, and how Stevie's sticky fingers had felt so trusting when they were clasped around her thumb.

Well, she'd been stupid, and she'd been stung. But she would never be that stupid again. In the process, she'd also gotten smart. She stayed away from men who were trying to get over past relationships.

Yet, she realized with misgivings, here she was, doing what she had promised herself she would never do again. She was listening to the anguished words of yet another man whose marriage had failed. And his story made her sad, which was not a good sign.

But as her spirits were doing a nosedive, Drew's were lifting. He had managed to tell her the worst thing that had happened in his life, and it hadn't been so bad. Always before, he had felt guilty whenever he told someone, as though it were his never being home that made his wife leave him, even though he knew better. He'd always felt the silent accusations, though, believing that if he'd been a better husband, he'd still have his wife and his daughter. Now, with Cathryn, he didn't feel the accusations, just her sadness. Sadness—for him? The thought that sorrow for his own misfortunes darkened her eyes like that, touched him very much. But there was more than sadness in her expression; there was a drawing away, and he didn't know why.

Just then a flashbulb popped in their eyes and they both snapped to attention. When the haze of whirling blue dots faded, Cathryn saw a well-known society photographer loping out the door, camera in hand.

"Ziff Bucholz strikes again," said Drew ruefully, staring after the retreating photographer. "I suppose we can look forward to our photos being splashed across the pages of *Palm Beach Parade*. I hope you don't mind." He regarded her anxiously.

Palm Beach Parade was the local scandal sheet, better known to Palm Beachers as "The Yellow Pages."

"It's all right," she replied, thinking that for once the pesky Bucholz, who found her photogenic and had annoyed her often enough in the past, had interrupted at exactly the right moment. She drained the last drops in her glass. "We'd better get back to the party," she said.

"I don't want to go back to the reunion," he said slowly, letting his eyes linger on her lips for just the briefest moment before meeting her gaze. "Let's sneak away and go somewhere else. Just the two of us, so we can talk."

"My friend Susannah drove me here tonight," she said slowly, wishing her heart wouldn't beat so erratically under his scrutiny. He was looking her over in a leisurely fashion, but not as a predator would; his eyes were lonely. In spite of herself, she wanted to melt, wanted to leave with him although all her instincts warned her against it.

"I'm going to go home with Susannah," she continued with effort, aching with it, yearning for him, wanting his fingers to linger upon hers again. Did her words sound as firm as she meant them to sound?

Drew laughed under his breath. "Susannah Fagan Atherton Smith LaMotte is currently surrounded by men who are competing to take her home. If you're counting on her for a ride, you'll be calling a cab." All seriousness gone, his tone was lazy, amused. He lifted smooth eyebrows, and his blue eyes twinkled. "On the other hand, if you go home with me, I'll deliver you right to your door. What more could you ask?"

Cathryn summoned every ounce of resolve in her body. "Thanks, but I'll pass," she said firmly. She stood up and waited for him to toss a few bills onto the table, then hurried ahead of him to the door.

She didn't slow her pace until they were outside, headed back toward the beach club through a fine spray of salt. Then, when they reached the shielding seawall, Drew stopped her by putting an arm around her and turning her so that she faced him. Her thoughts were suspended when she saw the emotion unloosed in his eyes, the precise curve of his lips delineated by the dim moonlight. Clouds skimmed their mist through his pupils, wide now.

"Cathryn Mulqueen," he breathed, his voice no more than a whisper, and her name on his lips became a harp song, rippling through her to her very soul.

He's going to kiss me, she thought, and she couldn't move. She stood, caught in time, in a web of his weaving, waiting for him to close the gap between them. She trained her eyes on his lips, avoiding his eyes—but, no, she had to meet his look. The message she read there told her that he wasn't kissing her casually, that he would want more, more than she wanted to give.

Slowly, he lowered his lips to hers, and she received their warmth with a sigh that became his breath, and then her breath, until their mouths were one. One of his arms curved around her small waist, pressing her belly to his taut abdomen, while his other hand traced its way up the smooth line of her back to her neck. He cupped her nape gently before threading his fingers through her abundant hair, cushioning her head as his lips deepened their caress.

His touch was reverent, respectful; he was no plunderer of womanhood. But he wanted her, tonight, desired her as he had wanted no woman except his wife. The way she responded told him that she felt the chemistry between them, and that was no surprise.

He stopped kissing her and drew her head against his shoulder, cradling it there, trying to think. He stroked the back of her neck gently, wondering if he should make a move now, longing to let his fingers stray to her breast, straining against his shirtfront. But if she really didn't want it, he would offend her. And he couldn't risk offending her, not now. He wanted something long-term and real, not something shallow and superficial. He'd had that, too much of it, since his divorce. With Cathryn Mulqueen he wanted more, much more.

And then he felt her shudder and begin to pull away.

"Not yet, dear Cat." he whispered, holding her close. "Just a few more moments like this. It feels so good to hold you."

"Please," she said, and her voice trembled. Where had the wind gone, and the moon? No seabird dared the silence that encompassed them, and the mist was not real.

"I don't want you to be uncomfortable about this," he said. He kissed her temple, and her eyes drifted closed at the touch of his lips. "I don't want to rush things." His voice was gentle against her hair.

"That's good," she said evenly, tilting her body away from his, imposing inches between them. "Because I don't, either." She had grasped control once more, had firmed her resolve into action.

He didn't like it, the way she knew how to freeze at will. His hands fell into emptiness, but not touching her was better than touching her and feeling the frost beneath his fingers.

"When can I see you again?" He wanted to sound tender, but instead the words were desperate.

"I don't think that would be a very good idea," she replied primly, drawing the armor of aloofness around her. Assiduously avoiding his eyes, she slipped like a wraith into the crowded beach club, leaving Drew stricken, staring after her. He wished she had been a figment of his imagination rather than a vital, breathing woman whose flesh had come to life against his, and who, for no reason that he could think of, had quickly turned and run away.

Damn, he thought, watching the fragment of a moon disappear beneath an enveloping cloud. He could have sworn he'd touched a chord in her, that they'd shared something special, even if it had only been for a few moments. He sensed a potential in her, a depth that he'd found in no other woman since his divorce. And having found it, he wanted more than anything in the world to explore it. Why was Cathryn Mulqueen so hard to reach? What did she have against him, anyway?

Heading for the bar, he thought he heard a sea gull jeer.

Inside, alone in the ladies' lounge, staring at her windblown reflection in the mirror, wondering if the wild-eyed and voluptuous creature staring back at her was her prim and proper, well-behaved self, Cathryn fairly gasped with the effort of pulling herself away from Drew. Oh, the attraction—she had never felt such a magnetic pull with anyone, anywhere. She never would have expected Drew Sedgwick, ex-football jock and team captain, to have such depth. She had known her share of shallow men, and she wanted no more of them. But, oh, the complexities, the structure of his mind, the shifting colors she sensed inside him.... Now, in the aftermath, she thought perhaps she should have let him take her home—to talk with him until the pearl-gray of the sky heralded sunrise, to inhabit the space of him for a few hours or even more. He would stop his pursuit of her now; she had lost her chance.

She had also lost her ride. The unreliable Susannah was nowhere to be found. She had probably decamped with Burl Cosworth, her steady boyfriend in eleventh grade, Cathryn thought.

Cathryn saw Drew once more before returning home, however. He waved at her jauntily from his bronze Porsche as she was maneuvering her full and flimsy skirt into the taxi.

Chapter Three

"His name is Avery Clark, and actually, it's pretty serious, I guess," said Susannah, nibbling at a morsel of Florida lobster dripping with butter. She paused dramatically. "We might get married." She lowered turquoise-painted eyelids.

"But what about Burl? You've seen seeing him every night since the reunion," said Cathryn. The two of them were indulging themselves at a farewell lunch for Susannah at Charley's Crab, a Palm Beach oceanfront restaurant.

"Oh, Burl." Susannah dismissed him with a careless wave of her hand. "He hasn't changed a bit. He's still a sloppy kisser."

"Susannah!"

"Good heavens, Cathryn, don't act so shocked. For an intelligent woman, you seem awfully out of it sometimes. Surely you can't be as conservative as all that. After all, you've been playing the field all your adult life, haven't you?" Susannah frowned impatiently and, seizing the bottle of white wine she'd ordered, splashed some into her glass. "More wine?"

"No," said Cathryn, waving the bottle away. "Wine only makes me sleepy if I drink it in the daytime. And I have to get back to work."

Susannah cocked her head. "Judy was right. You *do* work all the time. I couldn't stand it. Fortunately, since one of my husbands left me so well-to-do, I don't have to work." She frowned. "It was either number two or number three. Can't recall just which."

Cathryn sighed. "Then what do you do all day?" She couldn't imagine not working.

"Shop, read, visit my friends, look for available men. The good ones get scarcer every year, have you noticed? That's why Avery is such a prize. He's got black hair with these wings of silver at the sides, just like that guy with the winged hat in the Roman myths, Jupiter or somebody."

"It was Mercury," said Cathryn patiently.

"Okay, Mercury. And Avery has only been married once, and his kids are grown, which suits me fine because, you know, I can't picture myself being a stepmommy again, especially after my eye-opening experience with number two's little princess. Heather Marie. Lord, what a rotten kid she was. Insisted on sleeping at the foot of our bed on our honeymoon, and he *let* her, can you imagine? That's when I knew it wouldn't last. Anyhow, Avery has a house in Connecticut, a mausoleum, actually. It looks like his ex-wife, all dusty brocades and heavy oak furniture right out of King Arthur's court. If we get married, Cathryn, promise you'll come redecorate it for me."

"Sure," said Cathryn, figuring that the chances of ever actually redesigning the interior of the Connecticut mausoleum were nil. By next week, in all probability, Susannah would have found someone else.

"So how about you? Have you heard from Drew Sedgwick?"

Cathryn blinked. "What do you know about Drew Sedgwick?"

"What I read in *Palm Beach Parade*," said Susannah, pulling a copy of the local gossip sheet from her handbag. She flipped through the pages.

Cathryn was horrified to see herself on page 12, gazing raptly into the eyes of Drew Sedgwick.

"Ziff Bucholz," she murmured. "He jumped up and snapped that picture in the Alcazar Lounge right before we left."

"Nice picture," commented Susannah briefly before stuffing the magazine back in her purse. "Anyway," she went on, "I went to haul you out of the ladies' room that night after I figured Donny wasn't going to throw anyone else in the pool, and when I couldn't find you, I looked outside and there you were standing by the seawall and holding a very earnest conversation with Drew."

"Well, I had a drink with him in the Alcazar Lounge, as you already know. And that's all."

"How do you feel about him?"

"My, you do plunge right to the heart of matters, don't you?" hedged Cathryn, poking at a piece of parsley at the edge of her plate.

"The heart of matters. Of course," said Susannah, showing pearly-white teeth capped to perfection. "Oh, Cathryn, it's just that I think you need variety in your life."

"Like you have?" Cathryn couldn't help tossing off that remark, and Susannah just grinned.

"Not like I have. You're different from me, we both know that. But you can't go on like this. You need a personal life, someone to share your emotions with."

Susannah could get serious once in a while. Cathryn had forgotten.

"Look, Cathryn, give the man a chance. From what Judy says, he's a nice guy."

"If he's so nice, why did his wife leave?" retorted Cathryn, but she immediately felt like a traitor. It wasn't fair to judge Drew by his ex-wife's actions.

"There could be any number of reasons. The point is, why not give him a chance? I saw the way he looked at you out there when you were having your little chat outside. He was absolutely mesmerized. Surely you can see that."

Cathryn reached for the check.

"No, let me get that," said Susannah, but Cathryn held it out of her friend's reach.

"I should make you pay, just for having to listen to your lecture," she chided. "But I consider this business."

"Business? That's stretching it a bit, isn't it?"

"You asked me to redecorate that big old mausoleum of prospective husband number four's, didn't you?"

"His name, my dear, is Avery."

Cathryn laughed. "It's no use, Susannah. I can't keep your husbands straight any better than you can. I've converted to your numerical system, too."

As they strolled outside into the bright sunshine, Cathryn was touched when Susannah hugged her impulsively before ducking into her rented Cadillac.

"I meant what I said, Cathryn," Susannah said, her eyes dark and serious again. "Give Drew Sedgwick— or somebody—a chance. Promise."

Amazingly, surprisingly, Cathryn felt her own eyes fill with hot, unexpected tears. "But—"

"Oh, Lord, Cathryn, what's wrong? I haven't hurt your feelings, have I?" Susannah was aghast.

"No, no, I just—"

"Sh. Don't explain. Just promise you won't turn him down again."

Numbly, Cathryn nodded, too embarrassed to do anything else.

"Are you okay, Cathryn? Honestly? I hate to leave you like this."

"I'm all right. I was just thinking that I'll miss you when you're gone, you idjit." This, at least, was true. Next to Judy, Susannah was her closest friend.

Susannah brightened. "You always did call me an idjit," she said fondly. "And I always let you. Take care of yourself, okay?" Susannah settled into the seat of the Cadillac, her body sleek against the supple leather. "I'll phone you and let you know about Avery and me," she called out the open window as she backed the car out of its space in the parking lot, and again Cathryn nodded. She smiled—bleakly, she knew—and waved as Susannah disappeared down the street.

What in the world had come over her? Why had she been overwhelmed by such sudden tears? Was it the fact that Susannah, her old friend, surely sensed her loneliness and pitied her for it? Whatever Susannah had made of her own life, she was certainly not lonely.

Cathryn hadn't thought *she* was lonely, not before. She'd always had her work, and it had been enough. But if it was enough, why did she feel so sad when she thought about her life in comparison with Susannah's, with Judy's, with almost everyone's?

It was that damned reunion, she thought, resolutely heading back to her studio, determined to arrive promptly to consult with new clients about the redecoration of their home on Everglades Island.

Or maybe she shouldn't blame it on the reunion. In all actuality, her present state of churning emotions dated back to the night she had first seen Drew Sedgwick outside her Design Boutique, lounging ever so casually against a pillar in the shadows.

DREW BIDED HIS TIME. He didn't call her, forcing himself to stay away from her boutique in his Palm Beach Mall store. Instead, he embarked on an extended trip to California, hoping that business would help him push the image of her blond hair and green-gold eyes from this thoughts. It didn't help. He found himself thinking of her in the middle of important meetings, found himself seeing her in every platinum blonde who crossed his path. He even asked one of them out because her hair reminded him of Cathryn's. But compared to her this woman simply lacked charm and luster. By the time he arrived back in Palm Beach, he could wait no longer. When he disembarked from the airplane late Friday afternoon, he already had a plan. It was a little wacky, perhaps, but it was a plan nonetheless....

THE DESIGN BOUTIQUE was a raging success, both in terms of dollars and new contacts. Cathryn herself didn't have to spend much time there; her assistants managed it capably and well. In the month or so since it had opened, the boutique had netted her four big jobs. Two of them, houses in West Palm Beach, Cathryn turned over to Renee Bell and Zohra Vlast, designers who worked for her. The third, an office for an architect who could send plenty of business her way if he liked her work, Cathryn would handle herself. The other was a "handyman special" house on Pendleton Avenue, a run-down place that Cathryn would enjoy refurbishing and designing to the tastes of a young family.

Cathryn usually spent Friday afternoons at the boutique, going over receipts, approving plans, calling customers who had specifically requested to speak with her. On this Friday she lingered at the store until well after six o'clock, telling herself that the reason she stayed was that certain things required her attention. But deep in her heart she knew that wasn't the real reason. She kept hoping, Friday after Friday, that she would catch a glimpse of Drew Sedgwick. But she never did, and finally today, just before she left, she heard two secretaries from the store office talking about Drew's trip and wondering aloud when he would return.

Downplaying her disappointment, she let them step off the elevator ahead of her. *So,* she told herself ruefully, *you've been hanging around here every week waiting for Drew Sedgwick to show up, and he hasn't even been in town.* She felt like a fool. She had lost her chance with him, just as she'd thought the night of the reunion. Her promise to Susannah, that she'd give Drew a chance, was worth nothing if the man wasn't interested.

The sense of letdown stayed with her, a weight inside her chest as she walked to her car parked in the back of the huge lot. The heaviness didn't abate as she switched on the engine, flicked on the airconditioning, and slid a Linda Ronstadt tape into the tape player. She eased her Jaguar sedan out of its slot. A mournful Ronstadt song about love gone wrong played loudly, and Cathryn impatiently switched the tape off. She pulled the visor down against the glare of the hot April sunshine glinting off the chrome and polish of hundreds of parked cars. It was unseasonably hot for April, even for a south Florida April, and the asphalt of the parking lot fairly oozed with the heat.

She drummed her fingers on the steering wheel as she waited for a yacht to pass under the drawbridge to Palm Beach. The thought crossed her mind that she shouldn't be in such a hurry to get home. Nothing and no one waited for her there, and this bothered her tonight more than it had ever bothered her in the past.

Cathryn parked her car in the covered parking area beneath the exclusive Palm Beach apartment building where she lived. She stepped into the elevator and let it deliver her to the luxury penthouse she called home.

The first thing Cathryn did when she got inside was to kick off her hot shoes, chuck her panty hose into the nether regions of her closet, and wiggle her toes up and down in the plush white carpet. Next, she switched on the stereo, not caring what it played, as long as it wasn't something torchy. She felt lonely, and she thought of calling Judy. But then her mind flashed to the scene at Judy's house, where her friend was undoubtedly preparing a meal for Ron and Amanda, each of them telling the details of their day. This was family time in most houses.

But here there was no one to care about her day, no one to greet her and make her feel as though she had come home. The apartment seemed so silent and empty; was it always this way? Always one-dimensional? She'd decorated it to her taste, seeking harmony in space and form, but suddenly the lack of clutter seemed merely cold, the brass and gilt and glass hard. Why hadn't she ever noticed it before?

In the kitchen, even the bright colors of the framed Haitian primitive painting on the wall failed to cheer her. The shiny metal oblongs of the dishwasher, range and refrigerator greeted her like silent sentinels.

"Hi, guys," she said to none of them in particular, and she tugged at the door of the freezer until it swung open to reveal her choices for dinner.

Rectangular foil packages, bought by the dozen in the supermarket, were stacked in neat rows on the shelves. She ran through the contents rapidly. Lasagna? No, she'd eaten that last night. Skini-mini zucchini-and-rice casserole? No, she'd had that the day before yesterday—again.

She had just selected a chicken-and-noodle casserole and switched on the oven to preheat when the shrill sound of the doorbell startled her. Gurney, the doorman, was supposed to announce all visitors over the intercom before they came up, but lately the intercom had been out of order. Cathryn wished it had been repaired by now.

Slightly apprehensive, she opened the massive carved-cypress door cautiously, leaving the chain on. Through the small opening she was amazed to see none other than Drew Sedgwick standing there with a bottle of Veuve Clicquot in hands, grinning expectantly and looking exceedingly handsome in a short-sleeved knit shirt the color of his eyes.

"Cheers!" he said. "I hope I'm not too late for dinner!"

She stared at him, speechless, as the stereo played on, offering them a light Chopin melody as a backdrop.

"Couldn't you at least invite me in?" His blue eyes danced as his gaze swept across her face and to the room behind her. He saw a bar, long windows with a balcony beyond, a glass-topped gilt cocktail table.

She stood barefoot on thick white carpet, her shoe-lessness making her only slightly shorter than she had been in the store. Her height pleased him; he liked tall women, liked looking into a face that was almost on a level with his.

He couldn't stop himself from being curious about the way she lived, and he wondered if her natural habitat was decorated to be soft and warm or cold and inflexible—she was such an unpredictable combination, it had been impossible for him to guess. He couldn't get a feeling for the place from where he stood just outside the doorway; the only impression was one of luxury. He stopped looking past and focused on her face. Her eyes were wide and surprised, and he noted with interest that the irises were green rimmed with gold, not gold-flecked as he had originally thought. The gold rims put him in mind of picture frames, and he studied her eyes as he would a fine painting, trying to fathom the meaning behind them.

"What *are* you doing here?" she asked. "There's supposed to be a security system in the building with alarms and things. And a doorman."

"Your doorman is the father of Bud Gurney, the manager of our Palm Beach Mall store. Both Gurneys, junior and senior, think very highly of me. Say, do you have any champagne glasses? I'm getting tired of standing here holding this bottle."

Cathryn gave up. "Come in," she said. "It's hard to deny someone who is so persistent."

"Thanks," he said approvingly. "At last, persistence paid off. You know, I had no idea when I began all this that you were going to be so difficult."

He went to the bar at the other end of the living room while she stood motionless, watching him make himself at home in her apartment. He moved with grace and assurance, as though he would brook no objection.

"Do you always take charge when you enter someone's home? Most people wait until I ask them to—well, whatever."

He proceeded to pop the cork off the champagne. "No, I usually wait to be invited to—well, whatever. Only when I'm not sure I'll be invited, I find it's best to just charge ahead. How else could I get you to drop that aloofness?" His eyebrows lifted in a kind of shrewd impudence. With considerable finesse, he poured champagne into her hollow-stemmed champagne glasses and held one out to her. She had to walk around the couch to get it.

"So you find my manner off-putting," she said, playing for time while she absorbed the surprise of his being there.

"You know yourself that you're often reserved and self-contained, isolated in your own thoughts. Come on, admit it." His eyes riveted hers. The champagne in her glass wobbled, and he noticed.

When she was too startled to answer, he raised his champagne glass. "To designs," he said, whatever that meant. Still in a state of shock at his nervy invasion and at his equally nervy assessment of her, she raised her glass. She couldn't be angry with him, not when she'd spent the last few weeks agonizing over whether she'd ever see him again.

She took a sip of champagne, and then she remembered. "Oh, I've left the oven on!" She set her glass down on the cocktail table and hurried to the kitchen. Uninvited, he followed her.

His eyes took in the chicken-and-noodle casserole on the counter, the lack of any serious preparations for dinner.

"Would you like to go out to eat?" he offered quickly.

"No, thank you," she answered just as quickly. She picked up the casserole and pretended to read the directions, even though she knew them by heart.

"We might as well. We could go to—"

She shot him an impatient look, but her meaning was clear—no.

"We can hardly share this one tiny little casserole, can we? Do you have another?"

"Well," she said, reluctantly amused all over again at his persistence. No wonder he had succeeded in building up his department store chain from practically nothing. It was almost impossible to say no to the man, and he got his way without bulldozing. In fact, he didn't allow time to think of any objections before he accomplished exactly what he set out to do.

He opened the freezer door. "Quite a choice, I see. I'll have chicken-and-noodles, too—" and he tossed one of the aluminum foil containers on the counter next to hers "—and we should eat escalloped apples with it, I think. Oh, and here's a nice spinach souf- fle." He lobbed the containers one by one so that they slid across the countertop to rest beside the others.

"Drew Sedgwick, you're too much," she said, smiling at his performance.

"We'll set the table, of course," he said. "Would you mind digging out the best china while I put these in the oven? I thoroughly detest eating out of alumi- num-foil disposables."

Reluctantly adopting his festive mood, Cathryn gathered plates and silver from the china closet in the dining room and arranged them on the octagonal teak top of the dining-room table.

"Very nice," he said when he saw the table. He ap- propriated her arm. "Let's sit down in your living room and enjoy that lovely wide-angle view of the Atlantic. We have to finish our champagne." He grasped her elbow and guided her gently but firmly to the velvet couch.

The store, she thought in desperation, *that's what we can talk about. My boutique.* That seemed like a safe topic.

"The response to my Design Boutique has been ex- cellent," she said, keeping her voice businesslike. "I've taken on four big jobs as a result of it."

"You're a good drawing card. You've spruced up our usually sluggish spring sales, did you know that? Sales have gone up in furniture, in linens, in every de- partment having to do with home furnishings. People know who you are, so they stop in to see what's new in your section, and while they're there, they buy that new bedspread they've been thinking about."

"Then we're embarked on a venture that's mutually beneficial," she said, smiling at him, liking the way he so openly expressed his enthusiasm. Opalescent light from the uncurtained window, softened by approaching dusk, shimmered across Drew's features. His wide cheekbones swept up into startlingly blue eyes, which were long-lashed and expressively framed by wing-shaped brows. His dark hair glinted with blue-black highlights in the fading light from the wide window.

"And so," he said, after another sip of champagne, "tell me about your work schedule. Have you had to work even harder to keep the Design Boutique going?"

"I delegate most of the work connected with the boutique. I'm fortunate to have competent people working for me, so..." She gave a little shrug.

"That's one of the secrets, isn't it?" he said, studying her. "Hiring competent people. Sometimes it's hard to let them take over a job, though."

She nodded in agreement. "I used to want to poke my finger into every Cathryn Mulqueen pie, itching to see every swatch of fabric that came into the studio, pushing myself to dicker with every antique dealer. It isn't possible, of course, not anymore. My business has grown so big."

"Too big?"

"No, not too big. Not unwieldy. Yet I can't help thinking that I've lost some of the excitement that personal contact with every aspect of the business gave me."

Drew nodded understandingly. "I remember the first store I opened out of town. I used to lie awake nights, worrying that I couldn't handle all the day-to-day details. But everything fell into place, finally. I learned to save myself for wheeling and dealing and aggressively pursuing certain markets. Inventories, ordering, ad campaigns could all be handled by employees."

"You've been highly successful," she commented.

"So have you," he replied, turning the focus of the conversation back to her. He wanted her to talk about herself, to tell him about her business.

All at once Cathryn felt vulnerable and exposed beneath the gaze of those discerning blue eyes. Drew Sedgwick was a pretty good psychologist. He knew exactly how to wear down her defenses. This would be the time that most women would expose their hidden vulnerabilities; they would say, "Oh, but success isn't everything," and then go on to tell him in ways subtle and not so subtle how success had left them unfulfilled and wanting, had provided everything but a man. Well, she wasn't falling into that trap.

Instead, she sidestepped. "That was an interesting article about you in *Business Week*," she said, recalling the story that had appeared perhaps six months earlier.

"Not nearly as interesting as the article about you in *Palm Beach Parade*," he shot back. "Did the Sheikh of Isphat really give you a seventeen-karat emerald that you wear in your navel?"

In spite of herself, she felt her cheeks flush crimson. "I didn't know anyone with any sense read that scandal sheet," she managed to say. "And I don't remember the *Palm Beach Parade* article saying anything about an emerald. Even though I did design the interior of the Sheikh of Isphat's local residence, I can assure you that he never gave me a seventeen-karat emerald to wear in my navel or anyplace else."

He burst out laughing. "Well, that's a relief. A shame, though. You should wear emeralds. They'd do so much for your eyes."

"Where did you hear that ridiculous rumor, anyway?"

He laughed again. "I'm not about to tell you." He had her attention now; rumors about the illustrious sheikh abounded in Palm Beach.

"Drew! I can't imagine how such a story got started."

"Neither can I, especially when you act so prissy all the time. No one would ever, ever suspect Cathryn Mulqueen of wearing an emerald in her navel."

"I'm not pr—"

"Oh, but you are."

She set her glass down impatiently. "Look, first you stroll in here unannounced and invite yourself to dinner. You tease me with a ridiculous rumor and then become overcritical. What gives you the right to pull a stunt like this? The fact that I let you buy me a drink at our class reunion? Because we're business associates? I hardly even know you, and—"

"That's exactly the point, my dear Cathryn. I want to get to know you better. And you're not exactly the most receptive woman I've ever met." The troubled expression on her face worried him, and he softened his tone. "I want us to find out about each other," he said gently. "And we're a topic to be explored in a leisurely manner and with a certain amount of serendipity. Do you know what serendipity is? It's making fortunate discoveries accidentally."

What a line of patter! "I think I'd like another glass of champagne," she said, refusing to smile at him. She held her glass toward him.

So she was going to go all frosty on him, was she? He recognized her defense and refused to be daunted by it. There was a way to get around such things, and he knew what it was. It was an unfair tactic at this point, but if she wasn't going to be responsive to conventional tactics, he would have to see that she became receptive by another method. He had gone too far to be rebuffed now.

His eyes found hers and steadied them, and from this connection there grew a meaningfulness that she instantly recognized. *No,* she thought, this was not the way she intended it to be. She had always been able to turn men off with a look, a drawing away, a stiffness. It was something she had learned to do, attractive to men as she was. It was something she *had* to do to maintain her career as the most important thing in her life. Few men had ever breached this defense; few men ever tried.

Drew reached out for her glass, and his fingers against hers created a powerful surge of energy that embarrassed her, though she didn't know why. He gave no hint of noticing, however, and merely set both their glasses down on the cocktail table in front of them.

And then he was turning to face her, a soft expression playing across his face. His eyes, liquid and blue, caught hers, swirling her into their depths like a whirlpool from which there was no escape.

"Ah, Cathryn," he was murmuring close to her ear. She had no idea how he had managed to get so close. "There are certain things that we shouldn't leave to serendipity."

His arms went around her, tucking her against him, and she was aware of her own arms sliding around him, feeling the lithe strength of the muscles beneath his sweater. She wasn't ready for this, she told herself. She shouldn't be quivering in the warmth of his arms, waiting without breathing for what was sure to happen. She shouldn't be, but she was.

And then, purposefully, knowing exactly what he was doing, he touched his lips to hers, and it was as though the whole world opened out to pull in the light of the universe. She felt suddenly illuminated, although the room was growing dark, and the light that surged through her was diffracted as though she were a prism flashing rainbows everywhere. The source of the light was part of her, making her feel the differ-

ence between the soft, smooth moistness of his lips
and the rougher texture of his tongue, and he was
kissing her until the rainbows inside her blended and
circled and converged in a place she had never known
existed.

His hand cupped the back of her head, urging her
closer so that she could better taste the sweet tenderness of his mouth. She felt as though she were drown-
ing; she couldn't breathe, nor did she want to.

He was the first to pull away. She opened her eyes,
staring up at him, returning from the depths of her
rainbow fantasy. Surely he didn't mean to stop, not
now.

His hand remained on her neck, softly stroking,
disturbing the wispy tendrils. His eyes were lighted
with laughter, but not at her. They expressed the joy
within him, a joy he had somehow transmitted to her,
and she couldn't help but wonder at it.

"I'd prefer to go on kissing you," he said, his
breath warm against her skin. "But I think we'd better stop. According to my sense of smell, we've burned
the dinner."

Chapter Four

Wearing orange terry-cloth oven mitts on both hands, Drew plucked the little aluminum pans from the oven rack one by one and set them on top of the stove, assessing each one critically.

"They're ruined," said Cathryn, standing by and feeling helpless.

He regarded the chicken-and-noodles, blackened around the edges, and the spinach souffle, which actually didn't look too bad. A smoky crust edged the escalloped apples.

Suddenly Drew swung into action, delving into a kitchen drawer for a spoon, opening and closing cabinet drawers loudly.

"All we need is a bit of curry powder—ah, here it is—and perhaps some brandy. Do you have brandy?"

His enthusiasm was contagious. "Here's a bottle of Calvados," she said, producing the brandy with a flourish. "What else will we need?"

"A good salad, in case none of this works," he said, and their eyes met over the crisp remains of the escalloped apples and they both laughed.

Cathryn put together a hearty salad and tossed it with her homemade salad dressing. As she cut up the remaining carrots and tomato, she found that she was enjoying herself. Because of the untimely interruption of their scene on the couch, she would have expected things between them to feel strained or ill at ease.

But Drew didn't seem conscious of the fact that he had disarmed her so completely with only a few kisses. He hummed to himself as he spiked the escalloped apples with a swish of the Calvados, then tasted his creation.

"Want a taste?" he asked as she skimmed past, bearing the salad to the table.

"Later," she told him breezily, and he turned his attention to the chicken-and-noodles. Cathryn wondered if he was always so easygoing. His sunny nature, for her, was a pleasant surprise. Most men seemed to imagine themselves a version of Clint Eastwood playing Heathcliff, unforgivingly macho. They wouldn't be caught dead wearing orange terry-cloth oven mitts, although they might if they knew how attractive a little kitchen sense made them to women.

"Let's finish off that bottle of Champagne," she suggested, fetching it from the living room. She poured it as Drew finished tending to the burned casseroles. He deftly transferred them to the fancy serving dishes Cathryn had provided. She wondered if he'd always been this proficient with food or if the knowledge was something he'd had to acquire after his wife left.

She was lighting the candles in the dining room, the glow from the flaming wicks gilding her features, when he carried in the food from the kitchen. His eyes dwelled on her face for a moment before he wisely decided to keep the conversation light.

"Burnt offerings," he said wryly as they sat down.

"Not bad," Cathryn told him, testing her first mouthful of the chicken-and-noodles. "The curry seasoning almost covers up the burned taste."

"Try the apples," he said. "Don't you think the brandy adds something?"

"Definitely," agreed Cathryn after tasting them. "And the extra dash of cinnamon helps, too," she said.

They both sampled the spinach at the same time. They exchanged grimaces.

"I haven't figured out what to do about burned spinach souffle yet," he said. "Unfortunately."

"I have an idea," said Cathryn. "Throw it out."

His eyes met hers in the glow of the candlelight, and they sparkled warmly. She liked laughing with him, she thought to herself; she didn't laugh enough. She wanted to linger over dinner, watching the candles melt slowly down to their holders while she got to know him.

And then it hit her: she didn't want to have a good time; she didn't want to admit that he fascinated her. It would be all too easy to let this become more than it really was, to let it become an adventure in serendipity. The chemistry was there, a threat. Any emotional involvement would distract her from her work, and she was too dedicated to allow that to happen.

Not only that, she didn't know all the details of his past life. Drew Sedgwick was another woman's leavings, and this made her wary. Cathryn liked her personal life the way it was, quiet and uncomplicated. She didn't want to be hurt.

The smile on Cathryn's face faded, and Drew, in the mood to notice everything about her, noticed this, too.

"Why so woebegone?"

"Am I?" She tried to speak nonchalantly, but it wasn't easy, with his gaze probing her like that. It made her want to squirm in her chair, to bolt and run. She was not about to throw caution to the wind. Drew Sedgwick was still an unknown quantity.

The mood throughout the rest of their dinner was tense and edgy. Drew was aware that something had gone wrong; the expression on her face was like an echo of the night of the class reunion, when she had withdrawn and become suddenly remote. This evening she had been so absolutely open and passionate and delightful, just as he'd hoped she'd be, and he was confounded by the sudden switch.

That didn't keep him from trying to salvage the situation, however. He was a master of repartee, and he genuinely and lightheartedly tried to make it easy for her to respond to his banter. But Cathryn withheld herself from him warily, afraid to let him get too close.

After dinner, when they self-consciously and politely edged around each other as they cleaned up the kitchen at Drew's insistence, she thought he'd go soon.

"Show me where you work," he said suddenly and surprisingly after Cathryn had hung up the dish towel and latched the dishwasher door with a definite and final click.

"Well, I..." She hadn't expected this. She had been prepared to fend off amorous advances, but not an interest in her work. His genuine curiosity cast a spell; men seldom even cared about what she did for a living. "I do most of my work at the studio."

"The article in *Palm Beach Parade* painted you as a real workaholic who takes work home every night, slaving until the wee hours of the morning in your home office. Or is that as much of a rumor as the one about the emerald?"

She couldn't help smiling. "Of course not. I do work at home sometimes, but—" Then, her heart escalating at the leisurely way his eyes swept her face, she said, "This way."

She led him down the hall, still in her bare feet and wishing that she'd put her shoes on earlier when she'd had the chance. She could have used the dignity at that point.

Her home office was furnished sparely, in contrast to the luxurious furnishings in the other rooms. Drew appraised the room quickly, his eyes resting briefly on the desk crowded with paperwork, the slanted drafting table near the window. "It's not like the rest of your apartment," he said, restlessly exploring the bookshelves, scanning the titles, stopping once to take down a book and flip through it. He studied the framed and matted photos on the wall, professional photos of rooms that Cathryn had designed. Some of the pictures had appeared in glossy magazines like *Home Fantasy* and *Design Weekly.*

"I like my office plain, not fancy," she explained with a lift of her shoulders. "It's less distracting." His presence in the room dominated it; there was almost too much of him in this quiet, simple place. He seemed to shape the room to himself, to electrify it. She wondered if, when he left, he would leave some of himself behind and if she would feel him there when she sat down to work later.

"Do you work here every day?"

"Most days."

"And you work at night?"

"Most nights."

"And after you're through working?"

"I fall into bed, exhausted," she said. And she knew that his next question would be, "Alone?" but he didn't ask it.

Instead, as though afraid that the answer would be too painful, he moved his eyes away.

"What's this?" he asked sharply, inspecting a framed watercolor which hung on the wall.

"Just...a picture."

It was a seascape done in delicate pastels. The initials "C.M." were inscribed in the lower right-hand corner.

"Did you paint this?"

"Well, I...yes." She had given up painting years ago, although she had once entertained the idea of selling her paintings professionally. That idea had been driven out by her ambition; it had seemed more important to make a good living.

"It's very good. Do you still paint?"

She shook her head. "No. I don't enjoy it anymore."

"That's a pity. You have talent—but I suppose you know that. What *do* you do for fun?" he said, almost abruptly.

"My work is fun for me," she said carefully.

"You date?" A much more discreet question than the one he had wanted to ask.

"Sometimes."

"Anyone special?" His eyes pierced into her, trying to divine her answer before it was given.

"No, no one special." Her breath seemed to have left her lungs. Drew Sedgwick nodded, and for a moment a quiet elation lighted his eyes. His biggest fear—other than total rejection—was that she already had someone.

He turned away from her quickly and lightly touched the fuzzy leaves of an African violet in a clay pot on her desk.

"This needs water," he told her, and Cathryn couldn't help but notice the black hair springing up from the back of his hand, a minor detail about him, but now only one of many minor details of which she was much too aware.

"I—I hadn't noticed," she said, but she sounded anything but casual, and the words almost caught in her throat. Drew Sedgwick in her private place had an effect on her that she could never have foreseen; he was overpoweringly *there*, and her strong feelings about his presence disturbed and confused her.

She no longer saw him as a single impression, but viewed him feature by feature. He was gently tapered fingers; he was folds of suntanned golden skin at the elbows; he was a shadowed hollow of throat, a lean tendon beneath a jaw that seemed sculptured in strength.

"What kind of way is this for a woman to live?" he said sharply, jolting her out of her trance. "You're earning a good living, you could travel, enjoy life. Instead, you hide yourself away from the world and everything in it."

"You're wrong," she said, feeling an anxious surge inside her, wondering if it was from anger at his curt questions or from something else. "The world and everything in it are at my fingertips, waiting to be shaped into beautiful places for people to live."

"And in the meantime, the place where you live must be devoid of relationships, of people to make it real and warm and alive?"

This was not the usual kind of man-woman conversation, thought Cathryn despairingly. She had expected him to be curious and appreciative, and she was hurt that he was neither. Why was he delving so deep inside her, wanting to know about her? Why didn't he just leave her alone?

She didn't know what to say—this man made her nervous and unsure of herself, and she never knew what he was going to do next.

"You're retreating from me now, aren't you?" he demanded. "I can see it. You let your defenses take over, and the message is 'Leave me alone.'"

He knew. It was true, what he had said. She had always cloaked herself in a thin garb of reserve, letting few people penetrate it, and even the resulting loneliness was a kind of protection. But no one had ever had the audacity to comment on it.

He stood before her, his hands on her shoulders. His hands felt heavy there and strong. Her shoulders seemed fragile beneath them, bending under the weight.

She held her breath. She thought he would make his move, either invite himself into her bedroom or begin to impose upon her his considerable physical persuasion. But again, Drew Sedgwick surprised her.

"I'm going to melt that icy facade," he said mildly, a hint of a smile on his lips. At her blank and surprised look he said, "Oh, yes, Cathryn, I want to make love with you. But when it happens, it's going to be a conscious decision on your part, not just a spur-of-the-moment romp in bed. And it'll have to be something long-term, because I won't be satisfied with anything else!''

He dropped his hands from her shoulders, and she felt at once bereft. She didn't want him to go now, but he wheeled and walked to the door. She started to follow, but he turned and shook his head.

"I'll let myself out," he said, stopping her in her tracks.

She stood there staring at him. She felt caught in the frame of a movie that had just stopped inexplicably.

"I think the ice is already melting," he said, his eyes glinting in the harsh overhead fluorescent light. "Careful, don't let it drip on your toes. I wouldn't want you to get cold feet." Then, with a wink, he was gone, leaving her staring down at her naked feet.

THE NEXT MORNING, as was her habit, Cathryn pulled on her favorite pink warm-up suit and went for an early-morning run on Palm Beach. She seldom encountered anyone during these jogging sessions, but that morning she saw a swimmer out in the ocean, his arms slicing precisely and rhythmically through the calm water in a perfect crawl.

She jogged on until she reached the jetty, where she turned around, then headed back toward her apartment building. The swimmer was emerging from the sea, his skin slick and glowing in the light of the sunrise. She noted his regal bearing, his broad nose, his high, round cheekbones and full, well-defined lips—

it was Drew. She jogged five more steps, counting them. And then she stopped.

She wasn't prepared for the sudden lurch of her heart when she saw him wading toward her through the shallow water.

She smiled at him uncertainly.

"We can't go on meeting like this," Drew said melodramatically, pulling a towel from a waterproof carryall at the water's edge and drying himself. She watched him pull the towel down over his shoulders, recalling how his muscles had felt beneath her hands. A thick mat of hair covered his chest and stomach, disappearing into brief navy-blue swim trunks.

She reluctantly pulled her eyes away from his well-proportioned body, looking off toward the horizon where blue met darker blue at the seam of sea and sky.

"How did you know I'd be here?" she asked. Their meeting was too convenient to be an accident.

"Gurney senior told me that you like to jog early in the morning. I like to start out my day with a swim, and even though I've been swimming every morning in the pool at my apartment building, there's no reason why I can't swim in the ocean. In fact," he said, shamelessly running his eyes down her figure, "there seems to be every reason why I should."

"And what now?" she asked.

"I have an idea," he said quickly. "I know another beach where the jogging is great. Why don't you run on back to your apartment and pick up a swimsuit?"

"Drew, I have to work today. These new jobs I took on will take a lot of time and—"

"You work too hard," he told her seriously. "Didn't we agree last night that it's best to delegate some of the more onerous tasks? Besides, it's Saturday. You deserve some time off. I'm taking time off, aren't I? You should, too."

His arguments were good, very good. "Where is this other beach, anyway?" Without her realizing it, they had begun to walk toward her apartment building together. The towel around Drew's shoulders swung with each step they took; she avoided looking at it and at him.

"Hobe Sound. It's less than an hour's drive north, and I've got some property I want to check on, but I don't want to go by myself. You can come along for the ride; I'll bring food and drinks. And you may run on the beach to your heart's content, as long as you don't run away from me." When she dared to look up, he was looking down at her with warmth and affection, and more than that, concern. He really did think that she worked too hard.

She smiled up at him, thoroughly captivated by his caring. She never played when she should be working, and she always seemed to be working. For some reason, at this perfect moment on this glorious blue-and-gold beach, there was nothing she could refuse him. Suddenly her mind was made up.

"Pick me up in half an hour," she said. Then, tossing her fair hair back over her shoulders, she walked briskly toward her apartment building before she could change her mind.

The property Drew was going to check on turned out to be the beachfront house—quite an elegant and imposing place—that Drew had shared with his ex-wife.

"I moved out after the divorce," he explained as he turned his gleaming bronze Porsche off the ocean-front highway into the broad driveway shaded by two enormous banyan trees. "I found that an apartment in Palm Beach was better suited to my needs. But I love this house, and maybe someday I'll feel like moving back here."

Cathryn looked at the house curiously as Drew opened the heavy carved front door: cedar-shake roof, well-weathered by sun and salt air; St. Augustine grass, broad-bladed, clipped and edged, evidence of a gardener's expertise; tall hibiscus hedge with double red-ruffled blossoms; a spreading seagrape tree; a child's faded plastic beach ball, abandoned and forgotten behind a bank of wildly colored croton bushes. Wide-louvered shutters were tipped open at the bottom of all the windows, Bahamian-style. It was the kind of place she'd love to decorate; had he been serious when he'd mentioned that he'd like her to design an interior for him sometime? Was it this house he'd had in mind?"

Inside, the shutters let in light but not sun, creating a cool, shadowy interior. Furniture was shrouded by white muslin dustcovers, so that it was difficult to

discover anything about the decor. Spanish tiles felt
cool underfoot along a wide gallery; thick celadon-
green carpet cushioned her sandaled feet as they
crossed the living room. Cathryn couldn't help a bit of
rubbernecking, wondering if the furnishings reflected
Drew's taste, or his ex-wife's or a combination of
both.

Suddenly a scrap of bright red-and-white-striped
cotton fabric behind a chair caught her eye. Curiously she stooped to pick it up, sensing that it was out
of place in this formal room. It was a Raggedy Ann
doll, well worn and well loved. She turned it over in
her hands, then shot a questioning look at Drew.

Drew saw her bend over. He stopped with a pecu-
liar expression on his face and slowly, almost reluctantly, reached out to take the doll from her. His hands
held it carefully, gently, as he stared down at it. He
seemed unaware of Cathryn's presence, and very much
alone.

In the dim light of the shuttered room, Cathryn
found the feelings that flitted across Drew's face almost embarrassing to behold: anger, denial, grief. She
was an observant person. She had to be aware of
emotions and feelings in other people in her day-to-
day dealings with clients. She sensed that the emotion
on Drew's face was very real.

Neither of them spoke until Drew, with great effort, seemed to pull himself back to the present time
and place. He looked at Cathryn, almost as if he were
surprised to find her standing beside him. His eyes re-

vealed a raw suffering that she had not seen there before.

"This is my daughter's," he said, looking down at the Raggedy Ann doll helplessly. "Selby's."

The doll was a symbol, and it brought Drew up short at a time when he had been looking forward to what the day would bring. To what Cathryn would bring. The doll made him see that he still had a long way to go before he made peace with his past, before it was, once and for all, laid to rest.

He lifted his eyes to Cathryn's. She comforted him with her gold-green eyes, her expression deeply warm and sympathetic. An overpowering emotion, too strong merely to be called joy, grew in his heart.

He was no longer alone. Whatever inner battles remained for him to fight, whatever was required before he could truly outgrow his painful tragedy, he would have Cathryn. He didn't know how he knew this; he simply knew.

For the first time in a long time, the future looked bright.

Chapter Five

For Cathryn, the moment was fraught with uncer-
tainties. The way he stared at her, the impact of so
many complicated emotions flitting across his
face...she dared not analyze them, not here, not now.
She only knew that what he was feeling was intensely
private, unless he chose to include her in his thoughts.
What was important to her was that he felt something, and that he made no effort to conceal the fact
that he had feelings. Most men would have.

She attempted to bridge the moment with ordinary
conversation. She managed to speak quietly, calmly.
"Your daughter never asked for her doll? Never
missed it?"

"I don't know. I—I haven't seen her since she and
her mother left. It's been over a year."

A silence. "You must miss Selby very much," said
Cathryn carefully.

"I feel as though part of my heart has been torn
out," he said fiercely, and the anguish in his voice
startled her. But it touched her, too, this pained ac-

knowledgment. No, not the acknowledgment itself; what affected her so deeply was that he trusted her, felt close enough to her to open his heart to her.

There was nothing to do then but to reach out for him, somehow to share the pain. All the compassion within her welled up and went out to him, and her arms of their own volition opened up and clasped him in a strong and supportive embrace. He held on to her with a forlorn desperation as though she were all the things that he had been forced to relinquish.

His dark head bent toward hers, her warm cheek found its place against his. There was no evidence of sexuality in this embrace, only comfort. And although Cathryn was glad to be able to give this comfort, she felt even more relieved that this was a man who did not feel uneasy about receiving it. His arms tightened around her, as if drawing strength from her body.

"Let's put the doll away," he said quietly when they had held each other for a time, she didn't know how long. "Would you like to see Selby's room?"

She nodded. "I'd like that," she said, touched.

He took her hand in his and, holding Raggedy Ann in the other hand, led her down a long hall and opened the first door on the right.

In this room nothing was hidden by dustcovers; everything was clean and bright and ready, as though the room's occupant were only going to be out for the day and then return to sleep in the narrow bed as usual.

The room was decorated in a circus motif, with a parade of clowns and elephants dancing around the wallpaper border just below the ceiling. The spread was a handsome handmade circus quilt, and big, bright throw pillows were scattered about the floor for informal seating.

Drew set the Raggedy Ann doll carefully on the bed and looked at it for a moment before reluctantly pulling his eyes away. He led Cathryn to a framed photograph on the wall. It was of a little girl with glossy black hair and blue eyes, and she was laughing at Drew. She was perhaps six years old.

"This is Selby," he said.

Cathryn studied the picture. Father and daughter looked very much alike. In the long gallery she had noticed an oil portrait of a woman she suspected was Talma, but she'd averted her eyes when she saw it, so she didn't know if Selby resembled her mother at all.

"Selby's extremely pretty," observed Cathryn.

"Yes, she is. Of course, this picture was taken over a year ago. She lives in New York with her mother now. My ex-wife has refused permission for me to see her all along, and even though I have legal recourse, I feel that a custody battle at this time would be too difficult for Selby. We were very close."

He ran a hand over his eyes for a moment, then continued. "Her mother left me, presumably to pursue a career as an actress, but really to be with an actor, Alfredo Something-or-other, whom she met when he was working at the Palm Beach Playhouse. I'd give anything to have Selby with me; in fact, I'd prefer it, because I don't think Talma's a fit mother. As I said, I'm afraid of the effect a custody battle would have on Selby right now, so all I can do is negotiate to have her visit this summer, and I hope she will."

Cathryn nodded. "Then will you open up this house?"

Drew shrugged, and the sad expression behind his eyes grew even more intense. "I don't know. I suppose it depends on Selby. I'm not sure her memories of her final days here are pleasant ones. There was a lot of anger between Talma and me, and Selby cried inconsolably when we told her about the divorce. She was distraught by the time she and Talma finally left. Otherwise she never would have left Raggedy Ann behind. I wonder how Talma handled that; Selby wouldn't go anywhere without that doll."

"Perhaps Talma bought her a new one," said Cathryn, trying to inject a hopeful note. It moved her that this man, usually so ebullient, was allowing her to see him defenseless. There was no sense of his wanting her pity; there was no self-pity, either. There was just a trusting openness that was rare between two people, and humanness that was very endearing.

"Perhaps she bought her a new one," repeated Drew, although he didn't sound convinced. He drew a deep breath. "Well...this isn't why we came here, so that you could hear all my problems. Let's get down to the beach."

He took her by the hand again and led her through the dim house, and this time as she walked past the shrouded furniture, she almost thought she saw the slim line of a child's leg disappearing around a corner and heard the echo of a little girl's laughter in a faraway room. No wonder Drew hadn't wanted to come here by himself. The place was full of ghosts.

She breathed a sigh of relief when they reached a large kitchen. Sun flooded the room, stinging her eyes but chasing the shadows. Here all ghosts faded, and Drew, with an effort, managed to look more like himself.

Along the back of the house was a raised deck, screened and awninged and with a marvelous view of sand dunes and ocean beyond. Between the deck and the dunes grew one fabulous old scrub oak tree with wide branches that almost swept the ground in places.

"This is lovely, Drew," she said.

"I think so, too," he said. "Are you still in the mood to jog?" He slipped a casual arm around her shoulders, hugging her close.

"Not really," she admitted. She felt emotionally drained, and she suspected that he did, too.

"Let's take a blanket and lie on the sand, then," he said. "Do you need to change clothes?"

She shook her head. "I wore my swimsuit under my shorts," she said.

He looked down at the gauzy strawberry-red top she wore, at the white shorts, at her tanned legs and sandaled feet. She had worn her hair pinned up for coolness and comfort. "I must say, those clothes are better than that warm-up suit you wore this morning," he said with his old grin. "Where is it written, anyway, that joggers have to look like the Pillsbury Doughboy?''

"Joggers like to feel comfortable," she said as they strolled down the slope to the beach. She was grateful for his attempt at lifting their spirits. "And sometimes it's chilly on the beach in the morning."

"I know," he said. "Next time you're feeling cold, let me know. I'm sure I'll be able to think of some way to warm you up."

"Warm me up, melt the ice," Cathryn said with mock exaggeration, glad that their mood had taken a turn for the better. "You can't seem to talk about anything else."

"I can't seem to think of anything else," he said, helping her to spread the blanket and then pulling off his shorts and shirt.

She thought he would look away as she undressed, but he didn't. He watched with interest, but made no comment. Self-consciously she removed her shorts, feeling awkward under his gaze, and she sat down before she pulled off her gauze blouse. Lord, this was ridiculous, she told herself. It wasn't the same as undressing in front of a man, say, in a bedroom, and she suspected that if it *were* a bedroom, she wouldn't feel nearly as modest.

Stripped down to her white bikini, she settled herself beside him on the blanket, inhaling the sharp salt air, digging her toes into the warm sand. Little sandpipers scurried on matchstick legs ahead of the waves, looking for whatever it was they always looked for in the sand at the edge of the sea. Other houses, far apart, lined the beach, but she and Drew were the only people in sight.

Drew lay beside her on his back, his eyes closed, his face at peace, all traces of emotional turmoil gone. It amused him that she had been so inhibited about taking her clothes off. It amused him, but it surprised him, too. Obviously she wasn't used to putting on that kind of performance in front of a man, which he found reassuring. Despite her occasional coolness, he didn't think she was prudish; he had found her too passionate for that. But it was clear that she wasn't the kind of woman who spread her favors around indiscriminately, either.

Cathryn rolled over on her stomach, raising herself on her elbows. She had never seen him in repose before; always, he was filled with a dynamic energy that threatened to overwhelm anything and everything around him.

Drew's chest muscles swelled with a definition that made her want to reach out her hand and touch him. His chest rose and fell in a rhythm that seemed familiar, and she found that her own breathing, she didn't know whether consciously or unconsciously, was timed to his. His black lashes swept up, so long that they cast shadows across his cheekbones. What was it that she and Judy had done with their eyelashes when they were kids? Oh, yes, butterfly kisses. You batted your eyelashes against someone's cheek to give a butterfly kiss. Drew looked as though he would be very good at butterfly kisses.

She should have known that he would open his eyes and see her watching him, staring at him as though entranced.

"What were you thinking about just then—no, don't pull away," he said, reaching out quick as lightning and capturing her face with his hand.

"Butterfly kisses," she said.

"Butterfly kisses," he repeated, as though the words were foreign words and made no sense. His pupils expanded, blending with the irises in incredibly dark pools, and he tightened his fingers on her face before bringing her closer with the sheer magnetism of his eyes. Then his arm was around her, pulling her across the top of him, so that the hair on his chest touched her breasts just above the tiny bikini top.

Her left arm slid under his shoulder, easily and naturally. It felt right, and her other hand found a place on his chest. He said nothing, nor did she. Their eyes held, searched, found. In silent assent her lips parted and dipped toward his.

Against the inside of her wrist, she could feel his heart pulsate. His nipple stiffened and hardened beneath her fingertips, and easily, slowly she caressed it. When at last he released her lips with a low moan, she bent her head to touch his nipple with her tongue, sensing herself go dizzy with the feel of his chest against her lips. He eased his fingers through her hair until he found the pins and removed them one by one until the long, silken strands tumbled around her face and across his body.

His hands, gentler than she would have imagined, caressed her spine, pausing at the small of her back to tickle the sensitive spot there, then rippling tantalizingly away again. She felt her breath rising in gasps, and he drew her into a long, deep, satisfying kiss to which she responded as she had never responded to any other man.

There was no awkwardness in their movements, just mounting sensation sweeping over them in waves like the movement of the sea. The warm sun made them languorously slow; there was no sense of hurry or doubt.

Above him, the sun limned her in golden light, flickering around her bright hair. Dancing light shimmered through the curtain of her hair as it fell toward him, brushing his chest, and her eyes were liquid gold. He didn't mistake the desire reflected there, but understood the message that she found in him exactly what he found in her—consideration, caring, companionship and something more, something transcendental.

Excitement shot hot sparks through him at the thought that this woman, whom he had wanted for so long, who had held him lovingly when he couldn't control the pain of losing the two who had been most dear to him, that this woman wanted him. It seemed too good to be true, and her desire inflamed his own.

He found her lips irresistible, her breath sweet and arousing. He pulled her hard against him, stroking the nape of her neck as they kissed, until he felt her shudder above him, trembling before she let her weight fall on him, her full breasts crushed against his chest.

She tried not to tremble so, but she couldn't help but be overwhelmed by the grace with which he touched her, the sheer magnetism of his expression. She closed her eyes and reveled in feelings that she had not known existed. His mouth roamed to her ear, her throat, her eyes, her hair—seeking her out, touching, drifting, pleasuring its way to the top of her bikini, where his breath seared her skin.

She responded with passion he could hardly have imagined. He could scarcely resist tugging aside the insignificant triangles of fabric that covered her. But no, he could hardly do that here, although the beach was deserted now. Anyone could come along.

Her voluptuousness, new and startling, almost undid him. The thought surfaced in a flash, a burst of insight: was he falling in love with her?

He liked her, was fascinated by her, had longed to pursue her even when she gave him no hope. He knew with certainty that she belonged in his life. All that was possible without love. The deeply moving feelings he had for her were special and infinitely real—but *love*? The word encompassed so much that he was reluctant to attach it to any woman, no matter how much he trusted or cared about her.

He stopped kissing her, let his hands fall away from her smooth skin. The change startled her; her eyes opened, widened, and she softened upon recognizing the expression on his face.

The intense emotion displayed by his features amazed her, although afterward she would wonder why she felt amazement when his wonder mirrored her own. Tears stung the back of her throat, but they weren't unhappy tears. In a kind of awakening, Cathryn knew that she wanted this man, here and now, and he wanted her. And it was more than physical satisfaction that they both sought.

She wouldn't have dreamed that this could happen—everything that she believed was seemingly against such a situation developing. But all her fears had dissolved in those moments earlier when he had let down his guard; if he had been able to share his emotions with her, surely she could let down her guard, too. And he was still sharing emotion, an emotion so deep that she feared to give it a name, although she was familiar, vaguely, with this feeling. A few short months ago she would never have given in to it, but that was before she had found Drew Sedgwick. She'd never met a man like him before. He had proved to her without even trying that he was different—better—than all the rest.

"We can't stay here," he said hoarsely against her lips, making her body shiver against his.

"Where?" It didn't matter where, as long as it was private.

He wrapped his arms around her, tighter, tighter. "Not the house," he said, and she understood. "Come with me," he said, sliding out from under her;

their bodies were slick where they had rested against each other.

He stood up and pulled her with him, and deftly he lifted the blanket and shook it downwind. Then, his arm around her, he guided her toward the ancient scrub oak, sturdy and stout, thrusting wide, capacious earth-mother arms toward the sun.

A ladder led up the trunk; he went up first.

"A tree house?" she said, following and looking around. It was roofed and enclosed on three sides, with the open side toward the magnificant ocean view. Drew pulled pillows covered in bright cotton fabric from a locker and spread the blanket on the floor.

"A you-and-me house," he corrected her, pulling her down on the blanket beside him. He pressed her head to his shoulder. She blinked her eyes, getting her bearings. It was beautiful here, and quiet. The ocean, white lace spilling upon pink sand, provided the only sound, the cadence of the waves soft as a whisper. A gentle breeze cooled them, and leaves overhead filtered the sun and dappled their bodies with light.

It began again, the mingling of their bodies, progressing so naturally that it might have never stopped. They wore clothes, but the clothes disappeared somehow, and the surfaces of their skin were no longer separated by fabric. She felt lifted out of herself, unaware of the pillow under her head or the blanket beneath her. The only impression she felt was Drew—his gossamer, drifting touch, his warm, mobile lips exploring her body. His lips evoked sensations that she had never known existed, feelings she had thought she'd experienced but now knew she'd never really believed in until now.

His fingers shaped her breasts to the cups of his hands; his lips persisted in an exploration of her, seeing, tasting. The lovely rippling light played over his golden skin; the shadows brought out the blue-black glints of his hair. She moaned and moved with him, letting him guide her in the direction he wanted her to go, sometimes above him, looking down at him in rapt delight, sometimes beside him, pressed against the length of him, tingling where skin caressed skin. Beneath the blanket the curved boards of the tree house bent to the rhythm of their lovemaking.

She thought he would never part the smooth softness of her thighs, never touch the warm, wet moistness there. When he did, his fingers circling expertly to arouse her, she felt no hesitation about letting him see her own desire for him. He gazed at her, his half-lidded eyes sultry, drinking in her passion. His fingers continued to explore her, finding their way in a promise.

"Now," she breathed, thinking that she could stand the emptiness no longer, now that she knew it need no longer exist.

"Not yet," he said, taking his time, knowing that he pleased her by prolonging the exquisite sensation.

Finally, when she was sure she could no longer tolerate such delectable torture, he eased them together, pausing for a long moment to let her feel him filling her before moving again, gazing deep into her eyes with an expression of such caring that it moved Cathryn to the depths of her soul.

She had thought herself incapable of such wondrous emotions, sweeping her away, lifting her up and out of herself. She abandoned herself to his intensity, losing herself in it. His expert movements found the throbbing place inside her where her pleasure was greatest; she knotted her hands into fists and arched her back, experiencing a burst of warm waves, the rush of them hot in her ears.

Then he held her, let her spin down from that incredible high, and finally, slowly, gently, he raised her until she was sitting astride him. Still joined, they moved together until, with a hoarse cry, he reached his own heights. Their arms reached out, encircling each other, their salty bodies pressed close. Overhead, barely heard, a mockingbird trilled before it flew away, flashing its white-tipped wings.

Drew eased her down onto the blanket, arranging her so that her head rested on his broad shoulder, her hair curving across the dark hair on his chest. He touched her bright hair with his lips, tangled his fingers in one strand and drew them through it.

"When I saw you that night in my store," he said, his lips a mere whisper against her temple, "I thought you were the most beautiful woman I'd ever seen, with your hair gleaming in the dim lights and that distant, untouchable air about you. And then at the reunion, when you pulled away from my kisses, I felt more helpless than I've ever felt with any woman. I wanted you the first time our eyes met."

She tingled with the memory of the highly charged intensity in that moment of their meeting, when his eyes had first locked with hers—that openness revealing so much of himself in his first glance. And she'd never been more moved by anything than she was today by Drew's honesty about his emotions. His honesty had ennobled him in her eyes. So far, she had found nothing flawed in him, nothing that wasn't real.

"I can't believe my incredible luck," he said, and these were words that she had been thinking herself but hadn't had the courage to say. "I would have thought that you would be spoken for," he went on, his voice low and sweet beside her ear. "Why isn't there anyone else? A woman so beautiful, so intelligent—"

"I haven't wanted anyone—but then, I've never met anyone like you," she said, knowing that this statement made her vulnerable and therefore open to hurt. This time, with this man, she didn't care. Drew wouldn't hurt her. She didn't believe him capable of inflicting pain. He'd endured too much pain of his own.

Just before she was again whirled into the vortex of this still-unfamiliar pleasure, she had barely enough time to think that she had found him only so that she could lose herself in a new and frightening and fascinating way.

Chapter Six

Cathryn leaned back in her swivel chair, stretched her arms to the ceiling of her studio and yawned. It had been a long workday, abounding in canceled orders, back orders and an interminable phone call from one irate client who had decided she hated green, after insisting that her house be decorated in every possible shade of it.

Not only that, but Joseph Miles, an attorney for a reputable nationwide firm of interior designers, had called her long distance from Arizona with an offer to buy Cathryn Mulqueen Interiors.

"I've never thought about selling," Cathryn had said at once.

"As you know," the voice on the other end of the telephone had countered smoothly, "Designers International is acquiring small firms with a large share of their local markets. We've looked into your business and reputation, and quite frankly, we're impressed. My client would be willing to pay you quite handsomely. I'm sure we could work out terms that would be satisfactory to you.''

"Mr. Miles," she said impatiently, "nothing could be further from my mind than selling Cathryn Mulqueen Interiors. Sell? After working so hard? Of course not!''

"If you ever change your mind, please call me," Joseph Miles told her, repeating his telephone number once more. Knee-deep in more pressing problems, Cathryn had firmly put his phone call out of her mind.

Fortunately, such days did not occur often. If they did, Cathryn *would* forsake a career in interior design for something much easier—like driving a truck or digging ditches.

The staff of Cathryn Mulqueen Interiors was more than ready to call it a day. Cathryn heard her assistants Zohra and Renee chorus friendly farewells to each other as they prepared to go home, and she smiled at the friendly banter of her delivery crew, Jed and Elijah. And then it was quiet, except for her secretary's rustling in the outer office. Before long Rita poked her head in the doorway to tell Cathryn good-night.

"Good night, Rita," Cathryn replied with a weary smile. "Make sure you call Mrs. Brattigan first thing in the morning, okay?"

"Sure," said Rita, her gaze taking in the disarray of the papers on Cathryn's desk. "You'll be leaving soon, won't you?"

Cathryn shook her head. "I doubt it. I want to skim through these invoices and—"

"And you'll be here late. I know." Rita shook her head. She had been the first employee Cathryn hired, and she was fanatically loyal. But Rita didn't hesitate to speak her mind. "You ought to stop working these twelve- and fourteen-hour days," Rita lectured in exasperation.

"She's going to. I'll see to that." Drew's grinning face inserted itself into the space over Rita's left shoulder.

"Drew!" Cathryn smiled up at him; Drew's sudden appearance after a long, difficult day was like lifting her eyes and discovering a rainbow above the clouds.

"In that case..." said Rita, withdrawing with a bemused look.

They could hear her heels tapping down the corridor and then the click of the door latch as she let herself out.

Drew strode into Cathryn's office with a vigor and strength that she had learned was natural to him, and a look in his eyes that made her feel weak.

"So," said Drew, leaning over her desk, supporting himself on his knuckles, "another late night?" She looked so tired; he wished she wouldn't work so hard.

"I'm afraid so," she said, brushing aside a wispy strand of hair and liking the way his eyes blazed at her, blue as the heart of a flame.

"This isn't the kind of late night I had in mind," he said, standing up straight again and coming around her desk. "I had in mind something much more exciting."

"Such as?"

"Such as dinner, and then afterward we could go to my apartment. You haven't seen my place yet, and I *do* want you to design the interior for me. Besides, we haven't seen each other in two whole days, which is about two days too long."

"Drew, I—"

"No objections," he said firmly, lifting her out of the chair until she stood in front of him. He didn't release her but kissed her lightly on the lips, a kiss that lengthened and deepened until his arms went around her completely.

"I was planning to work tonight," she protested against his cheek.

"Consider this work," he suggested, moving away and smiling at her. "I'm a very important and particular client who wants his apartment decorated, and I can't wait. It has to be done pronto."

"Pronto?"

"Right."

"I certainly wouldn't want to lose a very important client."

"Of course not. So get your things and come along. When I hire an interior designer, I expect service." He understood her passion for her work; wasn't he basically the same way about his store? But too much was too much, and he was bent on convincing her of that.

She took her purse out of the bottom desk drawer and switched off the lights. The other offices were dark, and Drew whistled as he followed her down the long hall.

"Anywhere special you'd like to go for dinner?" he asked when they were outside on the Via Parigi, walking past the quaint shops, many of which would not open again until October, the beginning of the winter season.

"The café in the Esplanade? It's handy."

"Good choice," he said, guiding her elbow with his hand. She glanced up at him, proud to be seen walking on Worth Avenue with Drew Sedgwick. She felt that now-familiar wonder all over again every time she looked at him; she could still scarcely believe the happiness he had brought to her life.

Since that afternoon in the tree house two weeks ago, they had been together whenever possible in their busy lives—dinner, lunch, in between—and it still wasn't enough. She had thrown caution to the wind in her relationship with him, though she knew deep inside that she could still be sorry someday. But someday wasn't the wonderful and perfect now, and she was willing to forget that someday even existed.

Dinner was delicious, but Cathryn was glad afterward, when they were in Drew's car driving to his apartment building on the lake side of Palm Beach. She was eager to see the apartment; he'd meant her to, many times, but they had always ended up at her place.

"As I told you, it's a pretty basic apartment," Drew said as they rode the elevator up. "Ceiling, floor, four walls in every room. After Talma and Selby left, I was too demoralized to care about furniture or anything else, so my secretary called the home furnishings department at the mall store and told them to send over the bare necessities. But now that I've burst out of the blue funk I was in, I want something special, something nice.''

Cathryn waited while he unlocked the door. Funny, but her enveloping fatigue and exhaustion over the events of the day had dissipated. She felt fresh, eager, alive.

"It's three bedrooms, two baths, a dressing room," Drew told her, snapping on lights as they walked through.

"But the rooms are large, and the ceilings are high," observed Cathryn. "And look at the view of Lake Worth!" Across the water, the lights of the city winked on and off.

"I do like the view," agreed Drew, standing behind her, sliding an arm around her shoulders.

"Then we'll make the most of it," said Cathryn, letting her imagination take over. "And we'll add track lights in clusters to bring out the pattern of that magnificent marble fireplace, and we'll take up this carpeting and put down an area rug to define a conversational area in the living room. Maybe a few Egyptian touches, framed papyrus prints or something. Does all that sound good to you?"

"Anything you say sounds good to me," he said, pulling her closer.

"How about mirrors on the wall opposite the window to reflect the view?"

"I'd like that. Actually, I'd like anything you can do to make the place look more like a home. A place where I can have Selby visit and feel comfortable."

Cathryn's eyebrows flew up. "Selby? Is she coming?"

"I'm working on it. I want her to. But not to a place like this, a bachelor apartment. I'll want one of the bedrooms decorated just for her, but it has to be different from her room at the Hobe Sound house. When she comes, I want it to be a new start, with no memories from the past."

"Ah, I see." Cathryn thought for a moment. "How about something more grown-up than her circus room? A room that will take her through her school years to her early teenage years, if that's what you want."

"She'd like that. Twin beds, I think, so she'll have a place for overnight guests."

Drew ushered her to the room he had earmarked for Selby. It was a large bedroom with ample closet space, occupied now by nothing but a few cardboard boxes.

"I'd like to use beds with a half canopy," suggested Cathryn, warming to the thought of designing a room for a small girl. "Maybe we could put a dressing table on the opposite wall. I'll work up the plans myself, Drew. Then we'll look them over together."

"Okay. But you've got to promise not to spend time on it when we could be spending time together. I dn't want the work you're doing for me to be an excuse not to see me."

"Since when," Cathryn replied, kissing him lightly, "do I have excuses not to see you?"

"Not often," he admitted, taking her hand and leading her back to the living room. "But I don't want you to start."

She laughed and settled down on the couch next to him. He put his arm around her and she snuggled close, exulting in the pleasure of their physical contact. She had turned into a sensual woman with him, a woman who loved to be touched and stroked and kissed and made love to in every mood, every setting. Cathryn was astonished at the aspect of her personality that revealed itself when she was with Drew Sedgwick. She had not known that that Cathryn Mulqueen existed.

They had left the drapes open, and for several minutes they quietly watched the moonlight winding across the wide water, enjoying the peace of each other's company. This quiet peace was new, too. But it was good for both of them.

"When will you know if Selby can come?" she asked after a while.

"I'm not sure. It's hard, not knowing if it will work out. But it's important for me to have her here." Drew spoke vehemently, so vehemently that Cathryn sensed more than a father missing his child.

"Why?"

He was silent for a long time; Cathryn feared he wasn't going to answer. But then the words came out, slowly and thoughtfully, and she knew then that he had merely been framing them in his mind.

"I was raised by people who were paid to do it. I want better than that for my daughter, and when she's with me, I won't leave her upbringing to someone who doesn't love her. If Selby comes, it will change my life, Cathryn. I won't be able to work as hard. I'll spend most of my time at home with her."

She couldn't imagine Drew that way. No longer the hard-hitting, high-powered executive? Take his work away and what would he be? Who would he be?

"You look stunned." His eyes were on her, assessing.

"I am, in a way. You and your work—you *are* your work, Drew. I can't imagine you idle."

He laughed. "Idle? Raising a child leaves one anything but idle, Cathryn."

Flustered, she said, "Oh, I know. But you know what I mean."

His face became solemn. "I guess I do. My father was a workaholic, too, you know. The difference is that he slaved in that dreary store on Clematis Street year after year to earn a living for us. My mother worked with him. They hired maids to take care of me. Well, that store was the basis of my empire, and I'm not ungrateful. But I was lonely, and the housekeepers never stayed more than a couple of years at the most. I hardly knew my parents. I'd hate Selby to say, when she reaches my age, that she hardly knew me."

"I see," said Cathryn, because she did.

"And so that's why I work so hard now. Because I need to get ahead while I can, to become as secure as

I can, so that when Selby is here, I can afford the time off.''

"And what will you do then?''

"Let other people run the stores for me. Arrange my office hours differently. There are all sorts of things I could try.''

Quickly Cathryn related Joseph Miles's phone call and the offer of Designers International to buy her business. "Would you ever take them up on it? Ever consider selling?''

"Sell? After all the hours I've put into it? Drew, I've put more than just hours into Cathryn Mulqueen Interiors. I've put in blood, sweat and tears.''

"Why, Cathryn? Why do you do it?''

"Because I love my work. It's the reason, the only reason, and one that most people don't understand.''

Drew pulled her head onto his shoulder with a gentle hand. "I do,'' he said. "It's the way I was at first with the stores. Loving every minute, every problem, every solution.''

"Feeling good about yourself because you're accomplishing something,'' she said dreamily, feeling very much in tune with his thoughts.

"I was going to work and work, build something big, then sell the whole kit and kaboodle for a fortune and take the rest of my life off,'' he said reminiscently. "I thought Talma understood about the sacrifices. We were going to travel all over the world together, live anywhere we pleased because we'd be rich. Well, she decided not to stick it out. While I was out working myself to a frazzle, she found someone else."

"Oh, Drew, I—"

"Sh," he said softly, drawing her head back down to his shoulder. "If it hadn't worked out that way, I never would have known you."

"Which would have been too bad," she whispered against the graceful curve of his neck.

His finger beneath her chin lifted her head so that her eyes met his. His eyes sparkled at her across the space between them, and as his lips met hers, closing the space, she let herself relax in his arms.

"Too bad, indeed," he said against her lips. And then they didn't speak again for a long, long time.

OUT ON THE BRIGHT, SUN-KISSED WATER, the skier sliced across the wake of the speedboat, sending a high, glittering plume of spray into the air.

Cathryn, arms clasped around her upraised knees, sat with Judy on a bench beneath a tall Australian pine on the shore of Lake Osborne. The breeze from the lake sighed through the long blue-green pine needles above them, creating an illusion of an oasis of calm at the party. Today was Judy and Ron's tenth wedding anniversary, and they were celebrating it with a gathering of friends for beer, barbecue and water skiing on a Sunday afternoon. Drew was the water skier, and it was abundantly clear that he was skilled at the sport.

"Does Drew do everything as well as he skis?" asked Judy, crinkling her nose so that the freckles all ran together, and Cathryn sent her a sideways glance.

"Yes," she said, and the two of them laughed, still cohorts in a closed society. Then Cathryn became thoughtful and more than a little serious. "Drew plays hard and he works hard. He's a lot like me in that respect."

Judy produced a noise that, in anyone else, would have been described as a snort. "You mean working hard? I don't know anyone who works as hard as you do. I hope that in Drew you've met your equal."

"I think I have. It's not at all unusual for him to start his day at dawn and be at his office by eight o'clock. Then he works straight through until seven or eight at night and usually just has lunch at his desk."

Judy grinned. Cathryn's seriousness struck her as ironic. "Cathryn, you of all people should understand that kind of schedule. It's a wonder you even find time to see each other."

"I do understand, and sometimes it's hard to mesh our plans, harder than we'd like it to be. You know, I think Drew works long hours to keep his mind off his daughter. He misses her so much, Judy."

Judy craned her neck, searching for a sign of her own daughter, Amanda, in the group of children who were thrashing through the gaudy croton bushes looking for chameleons.

"I'd miss Amanda if she were gone," Judy said. "It's only natural."

"I suppose so. But with a man, I thought it would be different."

"That's where I think men have always taken a bum rap," said Judy. "Everyone assumes that when there's a divorce, it's easy for the man to be parted from his children. Easier than for the mother, anyway. I don't think it's true. Men love their kids, too, you know."

"Well, Drew certainly thinks the world of Selby. I'm glad, Judy. I'm glad he's not the type to walk away from the responsibility of a child. Selby is more than just a souvenir of his marriage."

"It does speak well of him," agreed Judy, shooting Cathryn a keen glance. The change in her friend was marked. She'd never seen Cathryn looking so satisfied, so relaxed, so...well, happy. But wisely, she didn't comment on her friend's new look.

Cathryn's eyes tracked Drew across the bright water. She couldn't watch him without thrilling to the way the muscles in his broad back rippled in the sun, without wanting to curve her fingers around the nape of his neck where they fit so perfectly. But this was not the time for that, she reminded herself. Here she would have to share him with everyone else until later. A hint of anticipation arose somewhere inside her; she could hardly wait until later.

The cookout rocked along at full speed. Judy and Ron's home, a big pool-and-patio house on the lake, was well suited to such gatherings, and Judy liked to entertain. Ron was a gregarious and popular land developer who had recently won a seat on the county council. Guests of all ages were queuing up for water skiing, pitching horseshoes and devouring hot dogs and hamburgers by the score. Ron had promised barbecued chicken by sundown.

"Whew!" Ron said, appearing from somewhere in the vicinity of the charcoal grill and wiping his forehead. "I think I need to sit down for a breather."

Cathryn and Judy edged over, making room for Ron on the bench. Cathryn liked Ron almost as much as she liked Judy. With his wiry brown hair and horn-rimmed glasses, he wasn't handsome in the classic sense, but he was the kind of person who was unfailingly pleasant and cheerful. Judy had married Ron soon after graduation from Florida State and, in Cathryn's opinion, she had made a good choice. Their marriage was stable, with a good deal of affection and caring, and they had been blessed with Amanda, a treasure if there ever was one.

"I think I'd better see how things are going in the kitchen. We seem to be doing a bang-up business in potato salad." Judy got up to leave, but Ron caught her arm.

"I know you like parties, honey," he said with a twinkle. "But on our next anniversary, I think we should throw our own party, just the two of us at some faraway resort with an exotic name and a private Jacuzzi."

Judy patted her husband on the arm. "Very good idea. Remind me of it when the time comes, okay?" She bustled away toward the kitchen, looking very much in her element as a hostess.

"So," said Ron, leaning back and reveling in the cool breeze from the lake. "Judy tells me that you and Drew are really hitting it off."

"Something tells me that we're in for one of our little chats," she said, smiling up at him. Ever since their days at Florida State, when Ron had started dating Judy and had fairly swept her off her feet, he had appointed himself Cathryn's unofficial big brother.

"We're long overdue for a little chat, as you put it," Ron told her. "Do you realize you haven't seen either Amanda or me for months?"

"You know how it is," she said. "I've had a lot to do."

"Still, it seems like the only time we see you anymore is when Judy shows us your picture in some highfalutin decorating magazine."

Cathryn laughed. "Come on, Ron. It's not that bad. Anyway, I've been seeing a lot of Drew, so it's not as though I've become a total hermit."

"Yes, and I'm glad you two found each other. Drew is a nice guy. He got a rotten deal from his ex-wife, and he deserves some happiness for a change."

"Don't go getting any ideas that Drew and I might be a permanent thing," warned Cathryn, although such ideas had crossed her mind more than once, only to be discarded when she realized that two workaholics would have a hard time being married to each other.

"You're both lonely, and you're obviously good for each other. Marriage is wonderful, Cathryn, and don't you forget it. Look at Judy and me."

"Everybody isn't like you and Judy, Ron," she said gently, thinking how, in contrast to herself, Judy really enjoyed all the things Cathryn thought of as housewifely occupations: sewing, cooking and cleaning. "Marriage might not be right for me. There's my career, you know, and—"

"Your career!" exclaimed Ron.

When Cathryn opened her mouth to object, he silenced her with an upraised hand.

"I understand how important your work is to you, but you should think about making time for other things. A husband and children, for instance. You can't imagine what a difference Amanda has made in our lives, Cathryn."

"I love Amanda, don't get me wrong," replied Cathryn patiently. "Not everyone is cut out to be a mother, though. I've never been able to reconcile the time it would take from my work, and at the advanced age of thirty-three, I've become a little less keen on the idea of having a child. Not to mention the fact that I'm one of those old-fashioned women who thinks one should have a husband first." She said this dispassionately. The fact that motherhood had passed her by—or more to the point, that she had so far chosen to pass *it* by—lost its importance long ago in the face of her success in her career.

"I guess what I'm trying to say is that you can't know what fulfillment is until you have a family to love. And to love you." Ron spoke earnestly, but Cathryn found herself wishing for a quick change of subject.

All this talk about marriage and children made her nervous. She and Drew had never touched on the subject, and it certainly seemed out of place to be discussing it now. Anyway, what did Ron know about the fulfillment of a home perfectly designed to suit its inhabitants, or the surge of satisfaction she had when she opened up her bank statements and saw that big dollar sign on the bottom line, knowing that she alone was responsible for it? There was fulfillment and there was fulfillment, and she had found hers.

She stood up abruptly. The speedboat had towed its skier to shore, and Drew was handing the water skis over to the next skier.

"Hey, I haven't made you angry, have I?" asked Ron anxiously.

She forgave him; Ron had been voicing his very real concern, and she was grateful that he cared enough to speak out.

"Not angry. Just impatient," she said with an understanding smile.

Ron looked relieved. "I don't know, I guess it's just the occasion of my tenth wedding anniversary. I want everyone to be as happy as Judy and I are." He looked up at her with an unabashed grin.

She patted him on the shoulder. "I'm glad you're happy. Just remember that happiness is different things for different people. You know, different strokes for different folks. There are Judys, and there are Susannahs. And there are Cathryns. And speaking of folks, I want one of them to try Judy's potato salad, and he's coming out of the water right now. I'll see you later." She headed for Drew, who by this time was drying himself off with a towel and looking about as though he expected to see her.

"Here I am," she said, surprising him by approaching him from behind and sliding her arms around his damp chest. "Want me to dry your back?" Her chin rested on his shoulder; she nuzzled his neck with her chin.

"You have the best ideas," he said, handing her the towel. She blotted him carefully, working in a few massages of the shoulder muscles as she did so.

"That feels good," he said. "Don't stop."

"Sorry, but I want you to try some of Judy's special potato salad before it's all gone. I think we'd better close in on the buffet table now if we want to get any."

They walked hand in hand up the slope of the lawn, carefully avoiding the area where people were slinging horseshoes.

"Nice party," said Drew, looking around him. He liked Cathryn's friends, felt a part of this convivial group.

"Ron and Judy always have nice parties. One thing I like about this one is that they've invited whole families, from grandparents to kids. It makes an interesting mix."

"Speaking of kids, I want to meet Amanda," said Drew. They loaded their plates with potato salad at the buffet table and sat down on a pair of lawn chairs. A group of youngsters playing tag barely missed running over their toes as they raced across the lawn.

"That's Amanda in the blue shirt, leading the pack," Cathryn told him. "The one with the short, reddish curls like Judy's."

"Cute kid. Say, this potato salad is delicious!" Drew dug into the potato salad, and Cathryn finished hers, leaning back in the comfortable chair and letting the sun warm her face.

This day had been fun, almost idyllic. As a matter of fact, the past few weeks had been wonderful. She and Drew had learned so much about each other, so much that was exciting and new. The more she learned about him, the more she loved him. Oh, yes, she loved him. She had finally admitted it to herself. There wasn't any doubt in her mind.

Drew—the sweet serendipity of discovering Drew. She had learned the feel and shape of him, the softness of his earlobes, the suppleness of his fingers, the rectangular shape of his feet. She had partaken of his gentle, lingering kisses until she felt replete with love, and then, to her surprise, she had wanted more kisses, and more.

Cathryn had learned to become uniquely selfless in their lovemaking, to be able to give more of herself than she ever knew existed. She and Drew had discovered and shared their qualities; together they were loving, giving, uncritical, reassuring.

The longer she knew him, the more confident she became that when the reality that inevitably intrudes on all lovers finally intruded on them, it would be something that they could handle. Her career, for instance. Cathryn's financial success didn't seem to threaten Drew. He was proud of her. And because she spent so much of her time immersed in her work, she didn't question it when he had to work late at his office. She understood the importance of the work ethic in his life.

Drew seldom dumped his problems on her or used her to shore up his ego. His ego didn't need shoring up. He accepted himself as he was and made Cathryn feel accepted as well. Cathryn considered them equals, and they both reveled in their wonderful companionship.

But marriage? They hadn't talked about it, and Cathryn didn't want to.

A pair of sticky hands slid around her neck from behind, and a pair of small arms hugged her.

"Cathryn!" said Amanda. "I've hardly seen you all day!"

Cathryn grasped one of Amanda's hands and pulled her around so that she could see her. "I know. I've been wondering where my favorite goddaughter was." Noticing Amanda's curious scrutiny of Drew, she said, "Amanda, this is Drew Sedgwick. Drew, this is Amanda."

The two of them grinned at each other.

"Why don't you get some food and eat with us?" suggested Cathryn.

"Okay. But I'm going to water-ski in a little while."

"There'll be plenty of time to ski before the sun goes down," Cathryn assured her.

Amanda skipped away and returned with a plate filled with potato salad, baked beans and pickles. She sat crosslegged at their feet. Drew watched in amazement as Amanda unconcernedly mixed her baked beans and potato salad together and placed the pickles on top.

"Won't that upset your stomach?" he said when he had recovered from the sight of it.

Amanda finished chewing a mouthful. "No, and anyway, the food will be all mixed up when it gets to my stomach, so I figure I might as well eat it just like this."

Cathryn stifled a laugh, but Drew couldn't. His laughter boomed out over the lawn, and Amanda looked self-consciously pleased.

When he was through laughing, Drew twinkled his eyes at Amanda and said, "Well, *my* little girl would have a colossal stomachache if she ate her potato salad and beans and pickles that way, I'm sure of it!"

"You have a little girl?" He had captured Amanda's attention.

Drew's and Cathryn's eyes met over Amanda's head. All at once Cathryn was afraid that Drew would find it too painful to talk about Selby.

But to her relief Drew said easily, "I have a daughter named Selby who lives with her mother in New York. She's seven years old."

"Will I get to meet her sometime?"

Drew smiled at Amanda. "I hope so," he said.

He found himself sending Cathryn a reassuring look so that she wouldn't worry that Amanda was probing painful territory. Cathryn responded with a smile that told him he had communicated his reassurance. It was always like that. They didn't need words.

Amanda finished the last of her potato salad-baked bean-pickle mixture. "What does your daughter like to do?"

Drew gave this careful consideration, and Cathryn knew that he was thinking that, after so long, Selby might have changed and liked to do things other than what she did when he had seen her last. But Drew said, "She loves to swim, and we go to the beach a lot. She likes me to read to her, too."

"Oh, she likes to be read to? I just love to read out loud. I could read to her if she comes to see you."

"She'd like that, and I would, too."

"Is she coming to see you soon?"

Drew was reluctant to answer that one, but he said, "I hope she'll be here this summer."

"Oh, good." Amanda stood up. "I have to go see how long it will be before my turn to ski. I'll bet it's *hours*." She skipped off toward the water's edge.

"She's a darling girl," Drew said, his eyes following her.

Amanda rushed back again for moment. "When Selby comes, will you take me to the beach with you sometime?"

"You bet I will," said Drew unhesitatingly, warmly, before she ran away again.

"You were wonderful with her," said Cathryn when they were alone again. The sun was sinking in the west; people were beginning to quiet down, finding places on blankets in the grass or in lawn chairs, where they waited for Ron's famous barbecued chicken to be served.

"For a moment, it was like being with Selby," he said.

They sat quietly for a while, watching the swimmers in the pool inside the big screened porch. Someone had brought out a guitar and was singing plaintive folk songs. The music sounded wistful and sad. Suddenly and urgently, Cathryn knew that she didn't want to hang around for Ron's barbecued chicken.

"I have an idea," she said softly. "Let's go."

"Go? Where?" Drew looked down at her, surprised.

"Anywhere where we can be alone."

Understanding, Drew's smile widened in pleasure and appreciation. He was pleased to know that she wanted to be with him, that their relationship took precedence over this gathering of friends. Cathryn was sensitive to his every thought, his every feeling, satisfying him as he knew he satisfied her. His heart swelled with love for her.

"You know what I love about you?" he whispered so no one else could hear. "I think I mentioned it earlier today. You have the best damned ideas in the world."

Chapter Seven

The next morning Drew awakened Cathryn gently by trailing soft breathy kisses from her shoulder to her throat. Sunlight filtered through the flowered pink chintz draperies of her bedroom, enveloping them in a rosy glow. She stirred and sighed, leaning into him, liking the way his body formed a warm nest for her. His toes wiggled against hers, a silent good-morning.

It began slowly, with none of the breathtaking passion that had marked their lovemaking of the night before. Now their love blossomed into a wonderful, slow eagerness, flowering quietly but surely, the way they knew how to let it happen. His hand caressed the curve of her abdomen; his fingers brushed lightly over her stomach and tantalized her breasts into rounded peaks.

She pressed her back into his downy torso, conscious of every part of him. They moved together, coupling, racing headlong together, until it all shattered in a ferocious joining, subsiding at last into sweet nothingness. They stayed linked together until their breathing returned to normal.

Afterward, he murmured to her, "If you offer to cook breakfast, I'll kill you. I hate breakfast."

"I know, but why?"

"Just the very thought of sending slimy eggs down to say good-morning to my stomach—"

"Please. Since you put it that way, it doesn't sound too appetizing to me, either. How about leftover veal stew?"

"Would you go for a frozen chicken-and-noodle casserole, like we had the first night we ate dinner together?"

She laughed, remembering. She rolled over in his arms, settling her head on his shoulder. It just fit, as though it were molded to the exact shape of his bones. Her hair, loose, unfurled across his arm, gleaming in the ribbon of light that escaped the draperies.

"I think," she said, tracing ovals around his navel, "that we should get out and jog."

It was a continuing argument: the benefits of jogging versus swimming. So far, neither had given in. Drew still swam every morning; she still jogged. Afterward, they met at the water's edge and sat and held hands until the sun appeared fully above them. They went their separate ways soon afterward, Cathryn to her studio, Drew to his office at Sedgwick's, sometimes taking time out from their busy days to meet for lunch, surreptitiously holding hands under the table and thinking they were fooling everyone, even though the shining expressions on their faces gave them away, and they saw each other almost every night for dinner.

"Did you know that jogging causes wrinkles?" said Drew, teasing her. "You should give up jogging. Swimmers never have wrinkles."

"Let's see." She slid on top of him, minutely inspecting his face. Not that she needed to; she had memorized it, every plane and contour. "Here's a wrinkle!" she exclaimed triumphantly, tweaking the skin beside his eye.

"Ouch," he said, trying to push her away. She clung to him with both arms and both legs. "You're awfully tenacious," he said when his efforts had failed. "Anyway, what I said about jogging was true. A wrinkle here—" and he nibbled at her neck where there was no wrinkle "—and here." He nibbled farther down, and the touch of his warm, wet tongue drew a gasp from Cathryn.

"You're tickling me," she said, laughing, pulling away. He wouldn't let her go.

"I'm going to do more than tickle you," he vowed, his hands sliding downward.

She curled herself into a tight ball and rolled away across the fine Belgian linen sheets. She landed on her knees and, hands on hips, laughed at him. "Last one ready to go is a—"

"If you so much as mention the word 'egg' in the morning, I'll—"

"Go ahead!"

And growling in mock anger, he was upon her. Then he was kissing her more and more passionately, and he was holding her as though he would never let her go.

"Cathryn, my love," he said, and she was dazzled, then humbled at the awesomeness of his love for her shining from his eyes.

An hour later, Cathryn assembled tuna salad sandwiches and they ate on her balcony overlooking the ocean, the salt breeze playing with their hair, riffling their clothes. The sky was a sun-washed expanse of blue above, and even so high above the beach, the rush of waves on the sand played a rhythmic music in the background. They were at ease with each other, their happiness heightened by their intimacy.

"You know," said Drew reflectively after a time, "I enjoyed being with Amanda so much yesterday." He chewed his sandwich thoughtfully.

"Maybe you could come with Amanda and me when I take her to the movies sometime. She'd enjoy that."

"Do you think she'd like to go to the beach with us? At the Hobe Sound house?"

"Why that would be lovely, Drew." Secretly Cathryn was surprised that Drew would offer this, as full of memories as the house was for him. Did he think that Amanda's presence might help to banish the ghost of Selby?

He must have read her thoughts, because he said, "Just hearing a little girl's laughter in that house again would be wonderful."

Cathryn reached over and covered his hand with hers, looking deep into his troubled eyes.

"You really do miss her, don't you?" she asked carefully.

"I'll always miss Selby when she's not with me," he said, a simple statement of truth.

"Have you heard anything more about her visiting this summer, or were you just being optimistic with Amanda yesterday?"

"Actually, things are pretty bad. You see, I've talked with Talma recently," he said, watching her carefully to see what her reaction would be.

Cathryn covered up a quick stab of surprise. He had not mentioned this before. She removed her hand from his and went back to eating her sandwich, sorting her emotions into a facial expression that she hoped came across as studiously casual.

"Talma's opposed to Selby's visiting. She says she won't have Selby upset by seeing me, and she claims that Selby is perfectly happy in New York. I asked to speak with Selby, but Talma wouldn't allow it. I threatened her with a court battle over custody, and we ended with Talma's screaming at me over the phone before she finally hung up." He disliked speaking of this; the dissension with Talma had worried and depressed him.

Cathryn's heart wrenched with sadness at Drew's obvious pain; then she was overtaken by a pang of jealousy of Talma. She chided herself about the jealousy. After all, Drew was here, with her, and she knew he loved her. Talma was of the past and far away. Why in the world should Cathryn feel jealous? She'd allow herself only the sadness, for Drew's sake. She hated to see him hurting.

"What will you do now?" she asked.

Drew sighed, and it was a troubled sigh. "My lawyer will talk with Talma's lawyer. It seems clear to me that I can't try to gain custody right now without proving that Talma is an unfit mother, and that seems likely to upset Selby. And I don't want to upset Selby, much as I'd like custody."

"Do you really feel that Talma is unfit?"

"I don't believe there's any doubt about it. She goes off for days at a time with Alfredo, leaving Selby with baby-sitters, and you know how I feel about *that*. Talma seems hell bent on pursuing life in the New York City fast lane. Drinking, wild parties, the whole bit. I'm going to have to weigh which would upset my daughter more—living in that kind of atmosphere or being torn apart by custody proceedings, where she's quite likely to find out more that I'd like her to know about her mother." His lips tightened, and his blue eyes darkened to the color of steel.

Cathryn paused for a moment, seeing the situation as a tangle of should and should-nots, coulds and could-nots.

"Are you sure custody is what you want?"

The hardness melted into an expression of emptiness. Drew looked as dejected as she'd ever seen him; his melancholy expression made her want to cry. "I miss my daughter. I miss her terribly. And if Talma won't let me see her, then gaining custody is the only way I have of having any influence on Selby's life. I want to be a good father more than anything in the world." It was important to him to express this to

Cathryn, the one person in the world whom he could count on to understand.

They sat for a few minutes in silence, watching a jet climbing up, taking off over the ocean. Drew sighed once more, the burden of his decision evident. Cathryn yearned to reassure him, to tell him that everything would be all right, but she felt so helpless in the face of his frustration. Everything might *not* be all right; they both knew that. It was the way of the world. But she couldn't help it—she wanted life to be perfect for this man she loved. The knowledge that she couldn't make it so curled into a tight, painful knot inside her.

She thought back to the day before, when Drew had so clearly and enthusiastically enjoyed being with Amanda. His positive feelings about fatherhood had been so obvious yesterday, almost as obvious as his present fierce longing to have Amanda with him.

"Oh, Drew," she said wearily, her heart aching for him. They fell silent again, but their communication still felt complete.

Drew roiled deep in his own thoughts, but it seemed somehow fitting to include Cathryn in them. There was so much involved with his longing to be with his daughter. His wish to be a good father harked back to Selby's birth, when his hope for his future was bright and untarnished by what happened later between him and Talma.

"I remember," he told Cathryn with a hint of nostalgia, "when Talma told me that she was going to have a baby. It was one of the happiest days of my life.

We had waited, you know, until we could afford a child. And the waiting was hard, because I longed to have a family, a family that would be different from the one where I grew up."

"You wanted a baby?" Cathryn's reluctant curiosity twisted inside her; this was a side of Drew about which she knew so little.

"Oh, I longed for a child. A little piece of eternity, that's the way I thought of a child. *My* child. And then, seeing her born—well, it was beautiful. That's the only way I can describe it. Beautiful."

Cathryn was surprised that Drew had chosen to be in the delivery room with his wife. "It's hard for me to picture you in the delivery room. I guess it simply doesn't jibe with the way I think of you," she said slowly, trying to imagine it.

Drew shrugged. "I was Talma's coach during childbirth, helping her with her breathing and so forth."

Another cold spasm of jealousy shook Cathryn over his sharing the birth of his daughter, *their* daughter— an important part of his life that Cathryn could never experience.

"I can't imagine that moment of birth. There's nothing in my realm of experience to bring it into focus for me." Cathryn spoke tentatively, trying to get a grip on it. She thought about the utter helplessness of newborns, of the thrill of hearing that first lusty, piercing cry of a tiny baby. She tried to imagine the purposefulness and the vitality of a hospital delivery room and couldn't. Her throat ached, and a kind of tension vibrated behind her eyes. She looked off into the distance to relieve it.

Drew's long look was filled with compassion. "I guess it would be hard for you to understand bearing a child. Just as hard as it is for me to comprehend how it would be never to have one. I'm sorry—have I brought up an uncomfortable topic?" He wished now that he'd never mentioned it; with his words she'd gone white around the mouth as though someone had slapped her.

She shook her head too vigorously. "No, long ago I came to grips with the idea that I might never give birth to a child. My career always came first. I never had time for marriage or motherhood. It was a conscious decision." If she spoke abruptly, she was sorry. Suddenly she felt sensitive about her nonparenthood, though she'd never felt defensive about it before.

Cathryn stood up quickly, her uneasiness erupting into restlessness. "I'll just clear away these things and—"

"We'll both clear away the dishes," said Drew, his eyes burrowing into her, knowing her. He sensed that the conversation had touched a nerve. Whether he knew that it was a newly exposed feeling laid bare by hearing him speak of his memories, she wasn't sure.

As she turned to go inside, her mind flew over the past weeks. During that happy and breathless time, with everything about their love so fresh and new, she and Drew had delighted in sharing everything. But now reality had intruded, as she'd known it would, although she couldn't have predicted that it would appear in quite this way.

Because of Selby, Drew's past would always be a continuing factor in his life. It was a part of him, now and forever, and he couldn't and wouldn't be able to walk casually away from it.

Sudden tears stung her eyes, but even the tears didn't wash away the ache in her heart indicating that the deepest and most meaningful human experience of all, the birth of a first child, would never be hers to share with Drew. For him, the experience belonged to someone else, and it always would.

In that instant she felt the first twinge of doubt. Her confidence in their ability to leap the inevitable hurdles that reality erected in the path of any relationship was severely shaken.

She knew that she loved Drew. And he loved her. But was their love strong enough to survive the future—and the past?

THE SUN, glazing the Hobe Sound beach with gold, formed the perfect backdrop for the flowing series of movements known as the sunrise salutation. Cathryn's body stretched to the sky and molded to the earth in the classic hatha-yoga postures, consciously relaxing in preparation for the new day.

She had awakened at dawn and slid from her place beside Drew without waking him. She'd dressed quickly in her canary-yellow swimsuit and hurried to the beach. She had grown to love the Hobe Sound house and its beach during the past few weekends they had spent there. Her fears about the progress of their relationship seemed to be unfounded. But then, she had to admit, since their discussion that day on her balcony, they hadn't confronted any more realities. They hadn't avoided them; it was simply that nothing had come up.

These weekends had been happy times, although at first Cathryn had felt guilty about taking time away from her work to be with Drew. Her guilt had disappeared when she realized that the love she shared with him became a reservoir of energy when she was away from him, and that she replenished that reservoir and enhanced her own creativity by being with him on weekends. Funny, she mused, how that worked. It was as though she absorbed something from their relationship, took in more than she gave. Cathryn had never worked more productively than she had since she had grown to love Drew, even though she was putting in fewer actual hours at the studio and in her home office.

Now concluding the sunrise salutation, Cathryn's body swept upright, her hands came to rest beneath her chin in the prayer position, and she instinctively felt Drew's warm presence behind her.

"You look like a lone flower on the beach, opening to the sun," said Drew in a tone of admiration. Every day with her, so special and so right, seemed like a miracle.

Cathryn's heartbeat quickened when she heard his voice. She opened her eyes and turned, smiling. She went to him at once, standing in front of him in the damp sand, clasping her hands behind his neck and tilting her face upward for his kiss.

"If I am a flower, *you* are the sun," she said, nuzzling his freshly shaven cheek. "Haven't you noticed that I'm phototropic—leaning toward you as a plant leans toward the light?"

"A romantic notion if ever I heard one," said Drew with an affectionate grin.

"I get that way when I'm with you." She tipped her head to one side, admiring the way his dark eyebrows framed his blue eyes so expressively. He winked at her before tugging his shirt over his head, then raced toward the ocean, where he disappeared with a quick dive beneath the surface. In a moment he was swimming parallel to the shore with strong, steady strokes.

Cathryn laced her jogging shoes on and began to run along the water's edge. Drew kept pace with her out in the water. She watched him swim, admiring his style. The high school athlete he had been was evident in his every stroke. She wished they had known each other better in those long-ago days. Would they have liked each other? There was no way of knowing.

She joined him for a swim after she ran. When at last they strode out of the water, droplets sparkled like diamonds as Drew shook them from his hair. She tossed him his towel and pulled a short terry-cloth bathrobe on over her swimsuit. They walked arm in arm up the beach gilded by sunlight, past the tree house with its memories, back to the house.

"Something to eat?" asked Drew when they reached the deck.

She shook her head. "you've talked me out of the breakfast habit," she told him. "How about a snack?"

"A snack?" Drew grimaced.

"Some fruit," she suggested.

"That's breakfast," objected Drew.

"It's a snack," she insisted, going inside to the kitchen and returning with an assortment of grapes, plums, peaches and bananas.

Drew nibbled on a grape. "If you call it a snack, it doesn't seem so bad," he conceded with a grin.

After they had eaten, he stretched and sighed. Then he pulled a tightly rolled paper from a basket beside his chair and, pushing aside the tray of fruit, unrolled a blueprint of the new Sedgwick Department Store that was being built in Daytona Beach.

Cathryn cleared away the fruit and returned to curl up in a big lounge chair beside him where she sat reading through a large stack of mail that she'd brought with her, knowing that Drew had work to do this weekend. The morning was balmy, although the day threatened to be hot. Drew stood at the table, leaning over the blueprint, marking changes on it with a red pencil.

When he finally straightened, he looked at Cathryn with affection. She never complained about his bringing work with him or interrupted his thoughts when he was thinking. He couldn't help but believe that she must be lonely, waiting for him to be able to walk on the beach with her or for him to be ready to talk.

"You know," he said, "we've never brought Amanda up here with us. I meant to."

Cathryn looked up from her mail. She loved Amanda, but she liked Drew's attention for herself. She valued these weekends alone with him, even when he had important things to do. It was a pleasure for her just to sit and read in his presence, with the gentle ocean breeze wafting over them and the shore birds calling softly overhead.

"I'd like to have Amanda with us sometime, but I'm glad it's just us," she told him.

"I thought you might be lonely, with me so busy," he said, gesturing at the blueprint. "Judy could bring Amanda up some weekend afternoon, and the three of you could visit while I work."

"I'm never lonely when I'm with you," she said.

Drew leaned over and held her face in his hand, smiling fondly. "What a nice thing for you to say," he said with feeling.

When his hand slid away, Cathryn tossed the stack of letters aside and stood up quickly, walking to the railing and looking toward the ocean. She wrapped her arms around herself and stood slowly massaging her elbows under the sleeves of her terry-cloth robe. What was wrong with her? He had been kind enough not to want her to be lonely, and he had suggested that she invite her favorite people in the whole world to assuage that loneliness. The complexity of her reaction puzzled her.

"Sweetheart, what's wrong?" Drew walked up behind her and placed his hands, comforting and steady, upon her shoulders.

"I'm not sure," said Cathryn unhappily.

She turned within his embrace and wrapped her arms around him, rubbing her cheek against the buttons on his shirt.

"Bear with me, Drew."

"Oh, I'll bear with you, all right. It's just that I don't know what's going on in your head unless you tell me. I'm not very good at guessing games." He tilted her face toward his and kissed the tip of her nose, his eyes reflecting his concern. He wanted to share everything with her, and he wished she felt secure enough in their relationship to confide in him.

Cathryn sighed and smiled. "Want to go for a walk on the beach?" she asked.

"Sure. I'm sick of looking at these blueprints." Drew slipped his feet out of the leather sandals he wore, and hand in hand they walked down the steps, past the big oak tree and to the dunes.

It was quiet for a Sunday afternoon; far down the beach a lone surf caster was fishing, and a pair of children whooped and hollered in the distance. Two couples lay on beach towels in a miasma of coconut-scented suntan lotion. They didn't look up as Cathryn and Drew strolled past.

Cathryn stopped to pick up a seashell, a spiraled shell of some sort. It was an inch and a half long, with a creamy surface striped artistically in shades of brown. Inside, she knew, its coiled interior was intricately whorled, shaped to shelter its former inhabitant. Today her own interior felt no less convoluted, no less intricate. And yet her interior—the way she was made inside—was meant to protect her, just as this shell was once protection for another creature. She slipped the shell into the pocket of her robe. Somehow, it seemed important to keep it.

"So what's the problem?" Drew asked finally when they were splashing along the edge of the water, getting their feet wet. Above them the sun shone brassy, bold. It was going to be miserably hot later on.

"Sharing you," she answered. She knew this sounded selfish, and it probably was. She knew it sounded unreasonable, too, but it was the way she felt and she wanted him to know.

Drew's eyebrows flew up. "Sharing me?"

She nodded. "I like being alone with you. I like it so much that I don't want anyone else around. I'm afraid another person would spoil it." This was said in a low, brooding tone, with her head bowed and her eyes averted.

"Cathryn." His voice demanded that she look at him, so look at him she did. He gazed down at her, his blue eyes liquid like the sea, love springing up from their shining depths. They had reached an outcropping of brown coquina rock, and Drew sat down on a flat, dry surface, pulling Cathryn down beside him.

He opened his arms to her and clasped her to his chest, so that she heard the sure, steady beat of his heart. It was reassuring, so rhythmic and strong, and

his arms around her seemed a bulwark against appre-
hensions and misgivings.

"Sweetheart, you don't have to share me with anyone. It's just you and me, even when we're in a crowd.
Don't you know that by now?"

Cathryn met his eyes, reading love and respect and
commitment there. She sighed.

"Oh, Drew, maybe it's not the sharing. It's the fact
that as long as we're away from everything else—the
telephone, people—we don't have to face the real
world. And its problems."

"What problems?" He looked genuinely puzzled.

She wanted to say, "Your ex-wife." She wanted to
say, "Your daughter." She wanted to say a lot of
things, but she didn't, because once she put them into
words, they could no longer ignore them, and for now,
for as long as she could, she wanted to hide from
reality.

He leaned his forehead against hers, his eyes deep
and dark and suddenly serious. "There's something
you need to understand," he said. "You've got to remember that I'm here to support you and care for you
and listen when you want to talk. The world and its
problems are something that you and I share, and
that's an aspect of sharing that you don't seem to have
thought about at all."

"Oh, Drew," she said. She didn't think he understood what she'd meant, because she hadn't been able
to tell him that the problems that loomed in their future all had to do with him and his past. And she

couldn't now that he had spoken so earnestly and from the heart, spoil this moment.

She slid her hands up his arms and around his neck, feeling nothing but gratitude for the kind of person he was. "I can't get used to having someone," she told him.

His arms locked around her as he buried his face in her hair. "Nor I," he said, his voice rough. "Nor I."

He kissed her gently on the mouth, and the poignant intensity of his lips communicated his utter involvement in her emotions. Her soul soared with joy; he cared about her. She had known, she *kept* knowing, but every time they touched souls again in a different way, she knew it all over again. Everything would be all right because he cared about her!

He lifted her to her feet, and she walked beside him back to the house, collecting her thoughts.

"The tide is rising fast," observed Drew, and she saw that their footprints going in the other direction down the beach toward the coquina rock were already obliterated. "And if I'm not mistaken," he said, shading his eyes with his hand and looking over the dunes toward the western horizon, "the wind is rising. We may have a storm before nightfall."

Cathryn looked, too, although she couldn't detect any rising of the wind. But she thought the sea shivered in the hot sun, and quickly, resolutely, she turned her eyes away.

Chapter Eight

By the next weekend, her mood had taken a turn for the better. Furniture for Drew's apartment had been delivered and the new lighting installed. Drew professed to be delighted with the change, especially with Selby's room, which Cathryn had transformed into a floral bower in pink and peony-red, with curtains of white organdy ballooned at the windows.

On Friday evening they drove to the Hobe Sound house for the weekend, as usual. As Drew turned his key in the lock, he said, "Seeing my apartment change before my very eyes has made me want to do something about this house, too. The house seems so different now, since we've been staying here on weekends. It's like a different place altogether."

"It's a lovely place, Drew," Cathryn said, following him inside. Because of the slanted Bahama shutters, it was still dark inside, but she didn't think of it as gloomy anymore. The weekends they had spent there—the nights making love and sleeping in the master bedroom, the days lounging on the deck and the beach—had purged the house of its ghosts.

She recalled the Saturday several weeks before when she and Drew had stripped the furniture of its muslin covers. They had come in from sunning on the beach one morning, and Drew had suddenly grasped the bleached muslin that covered a large chair and tugged at it until it slid off, revealing an armchair covered in a nubby white fabric.

"Help me with this, will you, Cathryn?" he said. "Grab the other side of the couch cover."

"What are you doing?" she asked, puzzled.

"You and I are going to be staying here almost every weekend, and there's no need to keep the furniture covered. I can't stand to look at rooms full of shrouded furniture."

"Oh, Drew, we spend most of our time on the deck or the beach, anyway."

"No, Cathryn, this is something I really need to do. I once thought that removing the covers, putting everything back the way it was when Talma lived here, would remind me of her. But now…" His voice trailed off as he stared down at her and she steadily returned his gaze.

Suddenly he strode across the floor to the wide window, where he yanked at the drapery cord until the fabric swept back from the glass, letting in more light.

Seeing that he was serious about this task, Cathryn said, "Okay, I'll take this end of the couch, cover, and you take that one."

"That's it," he encouraged, "we'll roll the fabric toward the middle to stir up as little dust as possible." Despite their care, they couldn't help raising little puffs of dust, and Cathryn's nose twitched at the musty odor of the upholstery. As she folded the dustcover, Cathryn tried not to look at Talma's wedding portrait smiling at her from the gallery, her heart-shaped face tilted to one side.

Drew relieved her of the heavy fabric and tossed it in a corner. And then, almost as though they were operating on the same wavelength, he hurried to the wall where Talma's portrait hung, removed it from its hook and stowed it in a nearby closet.

"There!" he said, looking pleased as he surveyed the room. "It's all done. I'd forgotten what this room looked like." He surveyed it with an air of satisfaction, pulled Cathryn close and kissed her tenderly on the forehead.

"You've changed the way I think of this place, Cathryn," he said. "You've made it cheerful again, a happy house."

Today, with the eye of a professional decorator, Cathryn took in the room's expensive furniture— contemporary mixed with rare antiques—an all-glass tabletop juxtaposed with a Chippendale sofa covered in a modern fabric, chairs upholstered in soft green, mauve and gray in a geometric print. The effect was charming and light in mood. And yet, some of the upholstery showed wear, and she'd be glad to help Drew choose new fabric.

"Let's go for a quick swim. Want to?" Drew, closing the big front door behind them, interrupted her thoughts.

"Sure," she said. "Just give me time to change into my swimsuit." She hurried down the long hall, carrying her overnight bag. Drew followed.

The master bedroom suite was big and airy, with a king-sized bed covered with a custom-made print bedspread that matched the quilted valances above the shuttered windows. Cathryn went into the large dressing room, with its multiple closets, and set her overnight case on the vanity. She usually hung her clothes beside Drew's in his closet when they stayed there, but at the moment he stood just inside the huge walk-in, rummaging on a closet shelf for his swim trunks and blocking her way.

There was no reason why she couldn't use the other closet, she reasoned, opening the door. She froze in amazement when she discovered that the closet was full of clothes, a woman's clothes.

There were dresses, some hanging in plastic dry-cleaning bags; shoes, neatly arranged on built-in shoe racks; handbags, each in its own cubbyhole.

She felt Drew behind her, and she swiveled her head, her eyes wide.

"Talma's clothes," he said in a quiet tone. "The ones she left behind."

This tangible evidence of his ex-wife's presence in the house where she and Drew shared a life on weekends hit her with a force that was almost physical. Doubts flayed her; she turned blindly toward Drew.

"I should have done something about them long ago," he continued, his voice low. "I didn't think about it." He was silent for a long moment, a moment during which she could hear every beat of her heart. Then Drew said decisively, "I'll pack up the clothes she left. She's out of my life for good, and I'm glad of it."

"It's not necessary to get rid of anything," said Cathryn stiffly. "I can use your closet."

"I want to," he said firmly. "I'll send Talma the things I think she might wear and donate the other stuff to Goodwill. You can help me."

"Oh, but Drew," she said, taken aback at the idea of invading another woman's—Drew's former wife's—closet.

"Doing this wouldn't bother you, would it?" asked Drew, brushing past her and then emerging from the closet carrying a pile of his ex-wife's dresses and dumping them across the back of the ornate low chair in front of the dressing table.

"These are Talma's things," she said, touching the top dress and feeling troubled. "She wouldn't want another woman pawing through them."

Drew stood before her, his hands loosely resting on his hips. He spoke briskly. "Nonsense. Talma took what she wanted when she left. She told me that she didn't want any part of me—not my money, my house, my love. Nor did she want the clothes I had provided for her, apparently. Although—" and here he laughed in grim amusement "—she didn't seem to mind hanging on to the various pieces of jewelry that I'd given her.''

Imagining the intensely unpleasant scenes that must have taken place between Drew and his ex-wife in this house, perhaps on this very spot, was emotionally more distressing than she imagined sorting through Talma's clothes would have been. Cathryn turned to hide her face from Drew, but the mirror over the dressing table reflected her anxiety and doubt, so that suddenly Drew focused his attention on her.

''Hey,'' Drew said, standing behind her and nuzzling her averted cheek. ''Try not to have hang-ups about this, okay? For my sake.''

She closed her eyes and rested her temple against his for a moment, aching over broken dreams and forsaken promises, none of them her own. No matter how much she loved Drew, no matter how soul-felt was her desire to help him find a new life, no matter how big a part she was to play in that life, she couldn't help feeling sorrow over a marriage that had ended. Even someone else's marriage.

Drew sensed the depth of her anguish. He turned her to face him and kissed her tenderly on the cheek.

''If this is going to be difficult for you, we don't have to do it. I'll hire someone to come here and clean the closet.'' Yet she sensed a reluctance in his voice, as though he didn't want to assign this highly personal task to anyone else. And suddenly, in a surge of understanding, she knew why Drew wanted to empty Talma's closet himself, and why he wanted her help.

She was silent for a moment, thoughts flooding her mind, overwhelming any qualms she had about the task. Now, with her, Drew was ready to leave his old life behind. Perhaps he had never truly been ready before, but he was now, and he wanted her to be instrumental in helping him to overcome the old painful memories. He wanted her to feel unmistakably a part of his new life. He wasn't being callous, or trying to subject her to an experience that would cause her discomfort; he was simply and of necessity trying to work past the old and get on with the new.

"No, Drew," she said, lifting her chin. "I'll help. I want to."

Their eyes locked in silent understanding before Drew turned again toward the closet.

They worked quickly and efficiently together, establishing one stack of clothing to be sent to Talma, another to be sent to Goodwill. Drew slid garments from their hangers and tossed them to Cathryn, who looked them over for imperfections. Anything that was in good condition and not hopelessly out of style was consigned to the pile to be sent to Talma. All other items were designated for Goodwill.

"What a lovely pocketbook," said Cathryn when Drew handed the tooled-leather bag out of the closet.

"I bought that for her," said Drew, running his eyes over it again. "We were on vacation in Spain at the time." He looked away quickly, as though it hurt his eyes to see it.

"Shall I put it on the pile to send to her?"

"I suppose so," he said, seemingly indifferent, but Cathryn knew better. She tossed the purse on the correct heap, then turned her attention to Drew. His lips were pressed firmly together, and he avoided her eyes.

She stretched out her hand and let it rest on his arm. "Drew, if you've changed your mind about doing this..."

He shook her hand away impatiently. "No," he said sharply.

She stood looking at him, hurt by his tone of voice and all at once feeling excluded. His face went soft when he saw the wounded expression in her eyes. He placed the scarves he was carrying onto the pile of dresses, then wordlessly gathered her into his arms. She felt his heart pounding beneath his thin woven shirt.

He didn't speak for so long that she was thinking of pulling away, of making light of the whole situation. She was glad that she hadn't when he finally spoke.

"Cathryn, forgive me. I didn't mean to speak so sharply." His voice was low and hesitant and muffled in her long hair. His hands opened and closed around the strands of it that hung down her back.

"Do you want to stop?" She spoke gently.

He shook his head. "We're through now. The scarves were the last of her things except for the shoes, and I'll ask the maid to pack them in the box with the other clothes she might want."

Cathryn was so filled with compassion for him that she scarcely realized the import of her next words: "You still love her, don't you?"

Drew's arms tightened around her until she could hardly breathe. Then he relaxed his hold on her and stepped away. His brow was lined; the tiny creases at the corners of his eyes seemed deeper than she'd ever noticed. He led her to the bed in the bedroom and sat down on the end of it, pulling her down beside him with an expression of uncommon intensity. His own eyes were deep pools, the pain inside him rippling up from their depths.

"I've asked myself that question over and over. At first, despite the fact that Talma went away to be with another man, despite all the unforgivable things she said to me, I wanted to forgive her. I longed to forgive her and get her back. Because at the time, she was all I knew. And if she came back, so would Selby, and I'd have my family again."

"And did you forgive her?"

"It wasn't that easy. But I did forgive her eventually. I thought for the longest time that if my love remained alive in my heart she'd come back. There's a lot of heartbreak in being left for another man; I suffered a lot of damage to my ego and my self-esteem. I kept punishing myself with the idea that I shouldn't have spent so much time at the office, trying to build an empire that was of no meaning and no use to me without her. I kept wishing that it wasn't true that Talma had left, that I'd wake up some morning and we'd all be together once more. It didn't happen, and slowly I began to mend. And then I met you."

Cathryn felt as though it would be too painful to draw another breath. She waited for him to continue.

He had never said whether he still loved his ex-wife or not. Cathryn's happiness, her certainty of his love for her waited to go up in a puff of smoke, ignited by the words she now fully expected him to utter: "I still love her."

Drew touched one hand to her face and slid it down the slope of her neck to her shoulder; he did the same thing with his other hand, his thumbs extending upward along the tendons in her neck. He could feel her racing pulse, she knew. She wondered if he could also feel the constriction in her throat.

"I met you," he continued, "and suddenly I wasn't thinking about myself—or my problems—anymore. I was thinking of you, of that soft light in your green-gold eyes when you look at me, of the way your wrist tapers so gracefully into your hand, of the laughter bubbling up from your throat in delicate waves." His eyes mesmerized her, so that she could look nowhere else.

"I love you, Cathryn. Believe it. I've found something with you that I've never experienced with anyone else—*anyone*. A depth of feeling and knowing another person beyond anything I ever thought was possible. I love you with every bit of life and hope and happiness in my body. Do you believe me? Do you?"

There was urgency in his touch now, and desperation. His eyes were intent and fierce, his look so compelling that she answered him truthfully and confidently.

"Yes," she whispered, because it was true.

He clasped her in his arms, lowering his head and kissing her, his mouth sweet upon hers but desperate with longing for oneness, for unity. And she responded with equal desperation, yet unable to abandon herself completely to the usually consuming passion, because he had not yet answered her question.

She opened wider, tensing in spite of wanting. Never mind the inner turmoil, she longed to give of herself to him. She could provide for him a way that Talma hadn't been able to; this was something she had to prove to him, to make him comprehend her love for him.

Loving was giving. Hadn't she read that somewhere? But she hadn't understood the true meaning of love until she'd met Drew, even though she'd had a remote abstract understanding of what it meant. Her mind raced along, thinking these thoughts despite the the touch of Drew's mouth, the feeling of his hands moving now to the buttons of her blouse.

She didn't want to think. She wanted to surrender to the feelings but couldn't. Not until Drew answered her question—did he still love Talma? She let her lips go slack, pulled away from him.

His eyes sought hers. His hand was still molded to her breast. "Cathryn?" he whispered. She had never hesitated in their lovemaking before.

She leaned farther away, back across the bed. In the deepening twilight, shadows in the bedroom faded into hues of purple.

She moistened her lips, dreading the question but having to ask it. "I asked you if you still loved her." The words hung in the emptiness between them, ready to fall.

Drew's eyes, darkest blue and shaded in lilac, embraced her. He took her hand. "I told you that I love you, and it's true. And I'm convinced that you believe me. So you must also believe what I'm about to say. I'll always love Talma in a way that no one else could understand. We shared our lives for ten years. She is the mother of my child. Even though we're fighting tooth and nail over Selby, I care for her because of these things. Can you possibly understand?"

Cathryn nodded. Her mouth felt dry. "I can try." The words were spoken hoarsely.

"But Cathryn, what I said before is true. I love you in a way I've never loved anyone else, even Talma. And believe me when I say that what she and I had at the time is over. I will never be *in love* with her again."

"You love her." The words fell like stones.

"I *care* for her. I'm not in love with her. God, I don't even like her very much!" Drew spat out the words, startling her, so that she began to comprehend his meaning.

She didn't know, couldn't know, what it would be like to be a part of someone else's life for ten years. It would be an all-encompassing experience. Living in tandem with another person would leave its mark. Drew's life with Talma had undoubtedly influenced him in ways that Cathryn couldn't fathom. As much as his childhood, as much as his adolescence, those years were part of him, had made him the tender, vulnerable person he was today—the person she loved so much.

She drifted toward him—her face, then her body. His hands were sure and knowing as he removed her clothing, and she found herself helping him, slipping out of her clothes with an urgency that she had never experienced before. When she lay completely naked on the bed, she shivered in the cool room, and he lowered himself over her, murmuring softly in her ear.

"Cathryn, Cathryn, my beautiful Cathryn," he whispered, his hands gliding like feathers up and down her body, eliciting the most tantalizing sensations in the deepest part of her. He raised his head, and in the dim light his features shimmered and she drew his head up to her level so that she could look into his eyes. At a moment such as this, his eyes wouldn't lie. He loved her, she could see it. With a deep sigh, she moved toward him until their lips met, letting their lovemaking draw a curtain of forgetfulness across her consciousness.

His lips softly brushed hers, opening and seeking. She tasted sweetness, and it seemed absolutely right; then the taste disappeared and she tasted what she had come to know as Drew, the essence of him. She had never much noticed what other men tasted like, and the thought that Drew tasted different intrigued and aroused her.

He stroked her thighs lightly and then more urgently until she opened them to him. Their union, when it occurred, was so complete and fraught with meaning that she cried out at the feel of him, and they moved frantically in unison, proving to each other and themselves in this physical act that their deeply felt emotions were true and real. When it was over, they remained joined, love and trust and joy once more renewed.

A long time later, when the walls had receded into darkness and all Cathryn could see was the outline of his profile against the moonlight from the window, she spoke drowsily.

"All those years of listening to people like Susannah talking about love," she said, nestling her head contentedly in the special place on his shoulder, "and I never knew it could be like this."

"I suspect that people like Susannah don't know what love really is," said Drew, turning his head dreamily to kiss her right temple. She snuggled closer, smiling into the darkness.

"Thanks for helping me with the closet, Cathryn. I know it wasn't easy, but it helped close a door in my life so that I can open new ones. I'm leaving the past behind, you see. And looking forward to a future with you. And with my daughter, if I can arrange it."

"What have you heard lately about Selby's visiting?" She asked reluctantly, but she had to know.

"My lawyer talked with Talma's lawyer last week, and Talma seems to be weakening about letting Selby visit. Talma wants to take a trip to Italy with her actor friend, and it would be difficult to take Selby along, so things look brighter."

For Drew's sake, she said, "I hope it works out." Yet, if she couldn't share him with Judy and Amanda, she wondered unhappily how she would share him with his daughter.

Drew stroked her hair, and his voice was low, melodious. "Selby's school will be out the first week in June, so I could fly to New York and pick her up that weekend. Although maybe I wouldn't want to come back here right away. I might stay in New York for a week or so, take Selby to the zoo, buy her some new clothes, get reacquainted."

She thought, then, that he would return his attention to her, because usually in the aftermath of their lovemaking, he was all hers with his sweet murmurings, gentle laughter, total peace. But instead, he went on talking about Selby, about how much fun it was to be with her, what a good sense of humor she had, and how much Cathryn would like her.

"Yes, that's what I'll do. I'll plan a little holiday, just for Selby and me." Drew's eagerness was growing, she could tell from the sound of his voice. "And then when we come back, you'll have a chance to meet her. You'll love her, I know you will."

"I'm sure I will," said Cathryn, but she felt a twinge of apprehension.

And yet, again, she mused, reality had reared its ugly head. She shifted her weight so that her head rested on the pillow, not on his shoulder. She forced herself to listen to Drew's voice with complete detachment while she pondered with encroaching uneasiness the addition of Drew's seven-year-old daughter into their lives. *If* it happened, that is.

Listening to Drew, only half hearing him now, she consulted her mental calendar. The first week in June—the week Selby got out of school—was only fourteen days away.

Chapter Nine

"You packed Raggedy Ann, didn't you?" asked Cathryn anxiously as her Jaguar negotiated the curving road leading to Palm Beach International Airport. She was driving Drew to catch his flight to New York for his reunion with his daughter. The visit and all that it entailed had come to pass suddenly, within the past week, when Talma had finally acquiesced to Drew's request for visitation. Cathryn wasn't sure that she herself was ready for it.

"Yes, of course," Drew replied. His own nervous energy was contained, but Cathryn knew that anticipation and excitement simmered just beneath Drew's calm exterior. He couldn't help the excitement; after all, soon, for the first time in sixteen months, he would see his daughter.

Heat emanated from the black asphalt road, and a stiff breeze whirled dust at the side of the pavement into miniature tornadoes. Ahead of them the airport buidings gleamed white in the sun. Cathryn drove distractedly, with an occasional glance at Drew out of the side of her oversized sunglasses. She hoped Drew was not aware of their secondary purpose: to hide her eyes in case she started to cry when they parted.

She knew that he was only going to be gone for a week, but his departure had taken on more significance than any ordinary leave-taking. Even though she kept telling herself that Selby's presence would not detract from their relationship, deep down inside Cathryn still didn't believe it. She'd managed to keep up a brave front with Drew, and she had tried to be encouraging about Selby's visit. She'd convinced him that she was looking forward to it almost as much as he was. But she hadn't convinced herself.

"I hope the reunion with Selby goes well," she said. It was the kind of thing she might have been expected to say on such an occasion, or that she might have said to fill in the silence.

Drew reached over and massaged her shoulder for a brief moment in quiet sharing. She was glad that Drew knew that she wanted things to go well, that what she had just said had been a heartfelt statement. He'd told her that the instant when he and Selby first were to see each other was one of his biggest worries. What if Selby barely knew him after all this time? What if she refused to go with him?

He removed his hand from her shoulder. She immediately wished he'd put it back.

"I'll use this week in New York to rebuild," said Drew. "I'll remind Selby of all the things we used to do together, like swimming and canoeing. I'll see how much she remembers of our lives together. Then I'll tell her how much fun it will be to do all those things again.''

Drew spoke with confidence, but Cathryn knew him well enough to know that he was still secretly anxious. She was glad he had remembered to pack Raggedy Ann. The doll would perhaps help to break the ice in those important first few moments.

''Do you think you'll have time to call Susannah while you're in New York?'' Cathryn asked him. They had discussed this, and Drew had agreed to phone their former classmate. Cathryn was concerned because although she had called Susannah at her apartment in New York several times, no one ever answered. Usually, if Susannah was going to be away from home for any length of time, she would let Cathryn or Judy know.

''I'll make time,'' Drew promised. ''Anyway, I'll enjoy hearing what our favorite scatterbrain has been up to lately. Do you think she'd like to go out to dinner with Selby and me?''

Cathryn shook her head. ''She's not terribly fond of children,'' she told him. It was an understatement.

''Then I'll make do with a phone call, and I'll make her promise to call either you or Judy pronto. Okay?'' He grinned at her.

''Okay,'' Cathryn replied.

She pulled the Jaguar up in front of the Delta terminal and a porter materialized to take Drew's luggage. Drew had only brought one suitcase and a small briefcase, however, so he waved the porter away and carried his own luggage to the check-in counter.

Cathryn stood to the side, feeling awkward, while he checked his suitcase. She hated airports; they were so cold and impersonal. They were designed for people who were going somewhere; for people like her, who weren't, there wasn't anything to do but stand around wishing she, too, had a destination.

Of course, the possibility of her going had never been mentioned. Not that she would have gone, even if Drew had invited her. She was planning to use this week as a chance to catch up on her neglected work. She was smack in the middle of rearranging the architect's office, and he was impatient to get the confusion of redecorating over with. During the past week, though, Cathryn had been so preoccupied with Drew that the architect's problems had taken a backseat to her own. But Cathryn did have a contract to fulfill and was becoming more and more worried that the architect was going to end up dissatisfied with the job she was doing. And he could, if he saw fit, do irreparable damage to her career.

"Hold this, sweetheart, won't you?" Drew thrust his jacket at her; the weather had been so hot that he hadn't worn it on the ride to the airport. She folded the jacket carefully over one arm, looking him over one last time to capture him in a mental snapshot.

For the trip he had dressed in a lightweight business suit and a white shirt, the same uniform worn by any number of other businessmen traveling to New York. But the way he wore it, with a certain ease and sophistication, set him apart from all the rest.

They had spent the night together, curved and enfolded in each other's arms. As Cathryn watched him, she felt a familiar yearning and then despair that he would be gone for seven days. The week yawned before her like an empty chasm, and she knew that no amount of work would fill it.

Drew hoisted his briefcase and turned to her with a smile. She held his jacket while he shrugged into it.

"I guess it's about time to board the plane," he said.

"I guess so," she replied, thinking that their words sounded so vacant and unfeeling. She wondered if Drew realized that when he returned with Selby, things would be different between them. She hadn't dared to talk about her fears with him in the past days.

"Take those sunglasses off, or I'll do it for you," he said, the catch in his voice belying his tension. "I want to see your eyes."

"You take them off," she whispered, her eyes never leaving his.

Slowly he reached up and lifted the sunglasses from her face; he did it solemnly, seductively, his eyes delving into hers. The earpiece tangled in a strand of her hair, and he twisted the frames to free them. She was spellbound by the pent-up passion in his eyes.

He couldn't imagine a whole week without her, and suddenly and irrationally he wished she were going with him. "I love you, Cathryn," he said hoarsely, and at that moment she knew that no matter how he longed to be with Selby, he hated being separated from her as much as she hated being apart from him.

"And I love you." The words seemed so inadequate for the deep emotion she felt.

They heard Drew's flight called over the public address system. He smiled, or tried to. "We're a little late. If it hadn't been for your wanting one more time..." A brief flash of humor found its way to his eyes.

"You were the one," she said, miming an attitude she certainly didn't feel. "Not even allowing me to take a shower in peace and privacy."

"Do you want to walk to the gate with me? Wave me off?"

"I left the car at the curb. There's a fifteen-minute parking limit, so I need to move it. Unless you'd like me to park it in the short-term parking lot and walk back?" They were being overly polite with each other; she hated public good-byes.

Drew shook his head. "There probably isn't time. I'd better get on the plane."

"Okay. See you next week." She tried desperately to be casual, even though her pulse pounded in her temples.

Suddenly he caught her against him with his free hand, smothering her face against the crisp gray fabric of his suit.

"I'll miss you, Cathryn. Take care."

The people bustling through the airport, the rattle of the voice on the PA system, the opening and closing of the doors as people came and went—all of it stopped. She clutched him to her almost violently, cursing the tears that rushed to her eyes and threatened to spill over. She pulled away, not wanting to spot Drew's coat.

Drew saw the tears. He put a finger gently beneath her chin. "It's only a week," he said comfortingly.

"Have a good time," she whispered. A tear formed slowly and trickled forlornly down her cheek. Others threatened to follow.

Drew nodded and tenderly kissed away the tear as his flight was called again; this time it was the last boarding call.

"I'd better go," he said hurriedly. "I'll call you from New York." He broke away from her, wishing she didn't look so sad. Suddenly it struck him, what she was going through. When he reached New York, he would have his daughter. Cathryn, left behind in Palm Beach, would have no one to fill the empty hours of his absence.

Cathryn raised her hand, waved. A group of tourists chattering in French wedged themselves into the space between them. Cathryn ventured a half-step forward, then realized the futility of it. Drew was far away from her now, striding in long steps through the terminal toward his flight.

A tremendous sense of sorrow washed over her, leaving her feeling weak and lost. She turned and walked slowly toward the outside doors. When she stepped out of the air-conditioned building into the humidity of a south Florida summer morning, it was as though she were being smothered by a warm, wet quilt. She felt stifled by the soggy heat, and she dispiritedly slid into her Jaguar, turned the key in the ignition, and eased the car away from the curb.

She adjusted the vent so that the car's air conditioner wafted its welcome cool air across her face. As she watched, a bright silver bird winged slowly up and away over the terminal building, sunlight glinting on its swept-backed wings. Drew was on that plane. She missed him already.

She couldn't help the sudden tears that rushed to her eyes just as she pulled out of the airport road onto the highway. Thinking about it later, she wasn't sure if it was the tears or the bulky sunglass frames that had blocked her vision. In any case, there was no way to avoid the blue pickup truck careening through the intersection past the yellow light, trying to beat the red.

Cathryn was never to remember the truck or the driver, just wildly squealing brakes, a harsh rending of metal and her own shock that this was actually happening to her.

"CATHRYN? CATHRYN! Wake up, dear. Open your eyes."

The command issued from an unfamiliar voice and was remarkably clear, considering that everything else swam through her vision in a blur. The pungent odor of antiseptic stung her nostrils. She blinked and tried to focus her eyes, wondering where she was and what she was doing. Nothing felt right; her arms and legs were icy and her head hurt.

No, her head didn't just hurt. It was excruciatingly painful. She opened her eyes again and dots spiraled through her field of vision. She was looking up at a water-stained acoustical ceiling, and when a body in a white uniform insinuated itself between herself and the dots, she realized where she was. She'd seen enough television to recognize a hospital emergency room when she saw one.

"Drew?" she whispered, but no sound came out. Then she recalled that Drew was gone, had taken a plane. Thank goodness, she thought. He's safe. The last thing she remembered was the crunch of metal. An accident. But Drew hadn't been there. She was thankful for that.

The head above her smiled a toothy smile. "Good. You're awake." A gentle hand patted her cheek and adjusted something on her forehead. "There. Is that more comfortable?"

Cathryn stared at her, willing her vision to cooperate. Her mouth felt unbelievably dry, and her lips had gone numb.

"You've been in an accident, dear, an automobile accident. I've called the name on the card in your wallet. Judith Carruthers? She's coming right over."

So they had called Judy. She swallowed, or tried to. "Who are you?"

"Emergency-room nurse. Don't lift your head like that—I'm still brushing the glass out of your hair." The nurse rattled a few instruments around on a tray before stepping from view behind the stretcher where Cathryn lay. Capable hands gleaned shards of safety glass from Cathryn's hair.

"You have a small cut, nothing serious. It'll require a few stitches, that's all. It's above your hairline—the scar won't even show. You have such pretty thick hair, it will cover it in time. In the meantime, we'll shuttle you over to X ray, make sure nothing important fell apart."

The nurse checked Cathryn's blood pressure, then removed the heavy gray cuff from her arm. Her arm prickled, as though not blood but soda pop flowed through her veins.

"Blood pressure's fine; your color's good. You take a ride up to X ray, and maybe your friend will be here when you get back." The nurse spared Cathryn a comforting little pat on the foot as two aides wheeled her from the room. Cathryn closed her eyes against the hazy pattern on the hospital corridor's ceiling as she was trundled along to X ray. She wondered if Drew's plane had landed in New York yet. She had no idea what time it was. But afterward, on the way back to the emergency room, they passed a wall clock, and she saw that it was almost noon. Drew's plane would be landing at LaGuardia Airport soon. *Good*, she thought, as relief washed over her in a wave. He didn't know, couldn't know, what had happened to her. And she didn't want him to find out. She didn't want anything to spoil his reunion with Selby.

Judy waited in the emergency cubicle until Cathryn returned from X ray. Concern was written all over Judy's pale face; the scattering of freckles across her nose stood out against her unnatural pallor. Cathryn's heart went out to her friend for the worry she'd caused her.

"They told me you were barely injured," said Judy in a shaky voice as she grasped Cathryn's hand in her own. "But I wouldn't believe it until I actually saw you for myself."

"I think it's just my head," said Cathryn, wiggling her toes experimentally. It was the first time since she had arrived in the emergency room that she had been able to manage movement in one of her extremities. Sensation was returning to her body, and her eyes had stopped whirling in their sockets.

She smiled waveringly at Judy. "How do I look?"

"Like someone who's been in an automobile accident," said Judy in obvious relief that Cathryn was talking and moving. "Like you won't be jogging for a while."

"Jogging? I should say not!" This emphatic statement was emitted from a newcomer on the scene, Cathryn's doctor, the same Dr. Folsom who had attended to her cuts and flu and vaccinations as she was growing up, and to Judy's as well. He was tall, but stooped and frail, and he had looked exactly the same for the past twenty years. Judy must have asked the emergency-room nurse to call him.

He tugged the cubicle's curtain closed behind him, and quickly he assessed the cut on Cathryn's forehead. In order to suture the wound, her hair would have to be shaved.

"We'll take off about a square inch, that's all," soothed the nurse, assembling a tray with a razor, scissors and a bowl of warm water.

Cathryn swallowed and fretted, but Judy, becoming her bubbly self again, now that she'd determined that Cathryn wasn't seriously injured, reassured her. "You can comb the rest of your hair over the spot, and no one will notice it," said Judy. Nevertheless, Cathryn closed her eyes as the nurse cut off the long flaxen locks at her temple.

"I took a gander at your X rays before I came to Emergency," said Dr. Folsom after he had sutured the cut and applied a small, neat dressing. Cathryn, still lying on the stretcher, reached her hand up and touched the dressing gingerly. It wasn't as big as she'd feared.

"Actually," Dr. Folsom continued, "you should remain in the hospital overnight for observation."

"I don't want to stay in the hospital," protested Cathryn. She felt more like herself now, and not so weak. But the cut was beginning to hurt, and her head throbbed. Her eyes beseeched the doctor.

"How would it be if I took her home with me?" suggested Judy quickly.

"Cathryn has had a concussion, and after a blow on the head such as this, we like to keep an eye on our patients. But since I know you both so well, I'd say it would be all right to take her home, either your home or hers. *If* you stay close to her, and *if* you report anything unusual in the way of symptoms." He eyed Judy sternly. "Do you think you could do that?"

"Oh, of course," replied Judy, placing her cool, comforting hand on Cathryn's forehead, a hand that was almost maternal.

Dr. Folsom signed a release form and cautioned Cathryn to take it easy for the next week, and after he left, Judy and the nurse helped her to sit up on the stretcher. Cathryn's head reeled for a moment, but then the world righted itself and she was able to ride in a wheelchair and transfer from it to Judy's Volvo station wagon.

"What about my Jaguar?" Cathryn asked hesitantly when she was tucked into the front seat with a light blanket across her lap. Judy started the motor of her own car.

"The nicest patrolman came into the emergency room just as I arrived, while you were in X ray. He said there really isn't so much damage, only a crushed fender. Ron's taking care of your car—don't worry about it. You were lucky; evidently the pickup truck barely glanced off the front of your car, and your head snapped forward and hit the windshield. The other driver wasn't even injured, just shaken up a bit."

Somewhat relieved, Cathryn rested her aching head against the back of the seat. She couldn't believe how disoriented she felt, how out of sync. The world seemed brighter since this morning, and it flashed by the car windows at a pace greater than Judy's steady speed of thirty miles per hour would indicate.

"You know," she said haltingly, "I'd really like to go home to my own apartment."

Judy shot her a worried look. "Really? I thought you could come to my house. I'd take good care of you."

"I know," Cathryn said, wincing as her head began to ache even more. "It's just that I'd feel so much better with my own things around me." She bit her lip. The emotional and physical trauma of the day were finally beginning to catch up with her. She ached, she missed Drew, and she wanted most of all to return to her own familiar surroundings.

"I suppose Ron could pack an overnight bag for me, and I could stay in your guest room," said Judy thoughtfully. "You shouldn't be alone."

"If you could do it, it would be wonderful. I can't wait to get into bed and sleep. My own bed." Cathryn felt perilously near tears.

When they approached the turnoff, Judy unquestioningly drove across the bridge to Palm Beach, and Cathryn found herself wondering how she would have managed if, back in fourth grade, she had gone ahead and eaten the cafeteria's canned spinach and thus missed out on her long friendship with Judy.

Chapter Ten

"If you'd like, I'll place a long-distance telephone call to Drew for you," said Judy, bustling into Cathryn's bedroom later, after Cathryn, wearing her best blue nightgown, was huddled in bed, looking pale and wan among the pillows.

"No!" exclaimed Cathryn, sitting bolt upright and startling Judy so much that she reared back.

Judy regarded her quizzically. "You *do* have his New York phone number, don't you?"

"Yes," said Cathryn, dropping her eyes and playing with the scalloped edges of the sheet. "He's staying at the Plaza. But I don't want you to tell him about my accident."

"Wouldn't he want to know?" Judy sounded incredulous.

"Drew would be so upset that he might cut his visit with Selby short," said Cathryn, raising her eyes again to reveal her inner pain. "And I can't let that happen. He deserves this time with Selby. I won't have it interrupted, when I'm going to be all right, anyway. By the time Drew returns, I expect to be good as new.''

"But, Cathryn," objected Judy with a puckering of her forehead, "that's not fair to Drew. Let him know and then *he* can make the decision about whether to come home early or not.''

Cathryn's eyelids fluttered and closed out of sheer weariness. She barely had the strength to talk. "I think I'll sleep awhile," she said, her voice trailing away.

Judy bit her lip and regarded Cathryn with a worried frown before slipping out the door.

Cathryn was glad that she didn't have to argue any more or further explain her decision. There was absolutely no doubt in her mind that she was doing the right thing, for Drew's sake.

Much later, the shrill ring of the telephone awakened her. She could have let Judy or her answering service take over, but she was positive that it was Drew. Her hand groped on the bedside table for the phone, and she answered it on the second ring.

"Cathryn," Drew said, his voice low and dynamic on the long-distance wire. "I miss you already."

She struggled to sit up in bed, wincing at the aches and pains. Outside it was dark; much time had elapsed since she had fallen asleep early in the afternoon. "I miss you, too," she said. She hoped she sounded normal. "Have you seen Selby?"

"I picked her up at Talma's apartment this afternoon." He paused, and when he spoke again, his voice trembled with emotion. "She's a terrific kid, Cathryn. She ran into my arms right away and buried her little face in my shoulder. I don't know how I'd managed to go so long without seeing her.''

"Is she with you now?"

"I've taken a suite here at the Plaza. She's asleep in the next room. Oh, we had a wonderful time this afternoon. We went to the Children's Zoo in Central Park, and I took her to a restaurant for dinner. Selby's a lot of fun. I can't wait for you to meet her.''

She was glad that he was enjoying Selby and utterly relieved that his fears about their meeting had been groundless. Drew had suffered enough emotional pain over his separation and divorce, and she had been so afraid that the meeting with Selby wouldn't go well, causing Drew even more heartache.

"Was she happy to see Raggedy Ann again?" Cathryn reached over and switched on the lamp next to the bed.

"Very. You know what she said? She said, 'Daddy, I thought when we got divorced, I got divorced from Raggedy Ann, too.' I had to explain that only Talma and I had been divorced, and that she'd always be my daughter. And that Raggedy Ann would always be her very own doll, no matter what. Evidently Talma didn't explain things too well.'' A trace of bitterness crept into his voice.

"How is Talma?" Cathryn said carefully. Her head pounded; she touched the gauze dressing on her wound to make sure that it hadn't slipped. She was careful not to let the pain edge into the tone of her voice; she didn't want Drew to guess that anything was wrong.

"The same. She's very uncommunicative, but at least she's cooperating about my visitation privileges, so I'm thankful for that. Anyway, she and Alfredo are leaving for Italy tonight. Enough about Talma. How are you?"

"Fine," she lied.

"Did you get much work done today?"

"Mm-hm," she said, at a loss. If they kept on in this vein, he'd suspect that something was wrong.

Judy nudged the door to the bedroom open and said clearly, "Is that Drew?"

Cathryn nodded her head but frowned and waved her hand, indicating that Judy shouldn't speak. Drew had heard her, however.

"That sounds like Judy's voice," he said.

"It is. I've asked her, uh, to spend the evening with me."

Judy, with an exasperated look over her shoulder, left the room. Obviously she still felt that Cathryn should tell Drew about her accident.

"I'm glad," said Drew warmly. "She'll keep you from being lonely. Is Amanda with her?"

"N-no, Amanda didn't come," said Cathryn haltingly.

"Well, since you have a guest, I'd better let you go. I just wanted to check in and tell you how well everything is going for Selby and me. And to tell you that I love you, my Cathryn."

"I love you, too," she said, meaning it as never before. For one wild moment she wanted to give in to her need and tell Drew about her accident. She longed to ask him to come to her as quickly as possible. She ached to feel the security of his arms around her, his soothing touch, his gentle kisses, but she wouldn't disturb his precious time alone with his daughter for anything in the world.

"Take care of yourself, sweetheart. I'll call you again."

"All right. Have a good time. And I miss you, Drew."

"I miss you, too. A lot. Talk to you soon."

"Good-bye," she whispered, and cradled the phone against her cheek for a moment before replacing the receiver.

"So what did Drew have to say?" Judy asked conversationally when she arrived bearing a tray of fruit and sandwiches for Cathryn's late supper.

Cathryn picked at a pimento-cheese sandwich. "He and Selby are having a wonderful time. She was really glad to see him."

"Well, I suppose so! How long has it been?"

"Sixteen months," said Cathryn before biting into the sandwich.

"I'm sure the separation hasn't been easy for either of them."

"No, it hasn't." Cathryn set the sandwich down on the plate. "I—I guess I'm not hungry. Judy," she said. "The sandwich is very good. I just can't eat it."

Judy's sharp look cut into her. "I don't think it's only the accident that has taken your appetite away. It's Drew. You miss him a lot, don't you?"

Cathryn didn't speak; she couldn't. And she was totally unsuccessful in masking the anguish caused by her own stubborn determination to keep her accident a secret from Drew.

"Let me tell him about the accident, Cathryn. I'll call him at his hotel. Just knowing that he knows—that he sympathizes and cares about you at such a time—would make you feel better." Judy implored Cathryn with her eyes.

"No," said Cathryn firmly. "I don't want him to know. Anyway, I already know that he cares about me."

Judy tried again. "Think how he'll feel when he arrives home and finds out what you've been through."

"No, Judy."

Judy fell silent for a moment, then her eyes came to rest on Cathryn. They were filled with worry. "I just want you to be all right, you know."

"I *am* all right," she said gently and deliberately. "Physically I'll be well on the way to recovery tomorrow."

"But emotionally?"

Cathryn didn't speak, and after a few moments Judy patted Cathryn's cheek thoughtfully, and silently switched off the bedside lamp before walking softly out of the room.

IN HIS SUITE at the Plaza, Drew sat quietly by the telephone, picturing Cathryn in her apartment with Judy. Cathryn would laugh, would smile, would toss her pale blond hair over her shoulders in the gesture he knew so well. In the gesture he loved so well.

He'd known he would miss her, but he had not counted on this hollow ache inside, as though something vital had been torn from him. In the long, lonely hours ahead, Selby would sleep and he would lie awake, remembering the night before when he and Cathryn had made love with such passion and such abandon, knowing that it was the last time for a week.

He stood and walked slowly to Selby's room, where he watched her sleep. His daughter. His child. He reached down and slid the sheet up to cover her bare arm, and he smiled as she frowned in her sleep.

And then he walked back to his bed, his lonely bed, and lay staring into the dark, thinking of Cathryn.

CATHRYN SLEPT WELL that night and awoke the next morning feeling mentally refreshed. But her body was still stiff from being jolted in the accident, and every joint ached.

Judy insisted on staying the whole day and the next night, too, even though Cathryn, who was beginning to walk around the penthouse, itching to get back to her work, was sure she didn't need Judy anymore.

"Nonsense," Judy said briskly. "I'm enjoying this. It reminds me of when we were roommates in college."

Drew called again that afternoon, and Cathryn regaled him with details of a make-believe day while Judy stood by helplessly, raising her eyes to the ceiling as Cathryn manufactured incidents that supposedly had happened to her while she was jogging on the beach and lunching with Judy.

"Honestly, Cathryn, I don't know how you can lie so easily," said Judy after Cathryn had hung up.

Cathryn stared at her unhappily, tears welling up in her eyes. With Drew, anything less than honesty cast a shadow on their love. The ugliness of her deception overwhelmed and saddened her.

Judy, immediately sympathetic, rushed to Cathryn's side and patted her caringly on the shoulder. "Sorry," she said awkwardly. "I shouldn't have said that, I guess."

Judy stayed through the next day, but that afternoon she packed her belongings, and she left after dinner. "I'll be back in the morning," Judy promised.

True to her word, Judy, concerned about Cathryn's being alone, stopped by to check on her the next morning and every morning after that.

"Don't tell me Drew Sedgwick has been nothing but a good influence on you," Judy had chided. "This business of skipping breakfast is disastrous." And with that, Judy had invaded Cathryn's kitchen, dredging up a griddle and frying pan and juicer, and prepared a breakfast so big that the two of them could scarcely eat it all.

"It's pure selfishness on my part," Judy said whenever Cathryn protested against all the fuss. "I like my coffee, and you would be back there in that office of yours working on who knows what if I didn't brew a big pot for us to linger over."

"You're not only spoiling me, but you're also making me lazy," said Cathryn on Thursday morning as she and Judy loaded the dishes into the dishwasher. She was still wearing her most comfortable bathrobe, and her hair hung loosely down her back.

"You deserve to be a lazy," Judy insisted. "I've always said you work too hard."

"Not lately. In fact, I've had several impatient calls from my client—the architect—who wants to know why there's a heap of plaster on the floor of his office."

"Yes, but admit it, this is the first time off you've had in months."

"Except for the weekends at Hobe Sound with Drew," said Cathryn, running those weekends through her mind like a videotape. Looking back on them, they seemed like such a carefree time. She and Drew had enjoyed each other's company, but at the expense of her work. Now that her refurbishing of the architect's office was running so far behind schedule, and after a few anxious inquiring phone calls from Mrs. Smead on Pendleton Avenue, she was beginning to wish that she'd spent more time at her studio.

"Well," Judy said, looking around the neat kitchen, "I'll see you tomorrow. Amanda's out of school now, so I'll bring her along. She's been clamoring to see you ever since the accident."

"Good. It'll be fun having her here," Cathryn said as she walked Judy to the door.

After Judy left, Cathryn tried to work, although it was hard to concentrate when she was waiting for the phone to ring. Drew's daily phone call had become the very pivot of her existence. She had not known, she reflected unhappily as she shuffled papers from one side of her desk to the other, putting off any real work, that she could miss anyone as much as she missed Drew.

The phone rang and she grabbed it. It wasn't Drew; it was her secretary, Rita.

"Another phone call from Mrs. Brattigan," she said. "She wants to know how soon you can get over there and do something about all that green. She says she can't live in the house without it making her sick, and she wants to choose the new colors right away so she can leave for Newport."

Cathryn pinched the skin above her nose with a thumb and forefinger. "Tell Zohra Vlast to drop whatever she's doing and to get over there tomorrow to smooth Mrs. B.'s ruffled feathers. And Rita, make sure everyone at the studio knows that I'll be working full time as soon as possible," she said feeling guilty about the many days that she hadn't worked when she could have. "I'll be another week or so at the most, I should think."

Rita sounded relieved, and after a few words of encouragement, she hung up. Cathryn sat brooding for a moment. She'd always been proud of finishing jobs close to the target date, despite problems with upholsterers and suppliers and furniture shipments that never arrived on time. She didn't want to develop a reputation for being undependable.

With a sigh, she went to her drawing board and, working quickly, mapped out a recreation room for the Pendleton Avenue house. Becoming absorbed in her task, she soon discovered there was space for a pool table in the room after all. She'd have one specially fitted with orange baize instead of the usual golf-course green. Orange was Mr. Smead's favorite color.

When Drew finally phoned, the conversation was kept short by Selby's constant calls for attention. It was just as well, Cathryn thought. Her work was distracting her, and she couldn't have maintained the deception that all was well with her any longer.

"How are you doing?" he said.

"Fine," she told him. She had to bite her lip to keep from blurting out the truth.

"Almost finished with the architect's office? Does he like those textured solar-screen blinds you found for the big windows in his reception room?"

"Loves them," she said.

"Not as much as I love you," he shot back.

Cathryn didn't speak; she couldn't force words past the lump in her throat. She should have come up with some pert rejoinder, should have made some sound of agreement. She yearned to tell him that she loved him, but she wasn't able to. She seemed to be sinking into some sort of post-accident depression, growing more lethargic every day.

The silence lengthened, became obvious. *I've got to think of something to say,* she thought desperately. *Something funny, something silly, something that will make him think everything is all right*. Only she couldn't think of a thing.

Then Selby laughed in the background and spoke to Drew, and he covered the mouthpiece with his hand. Cathryn heard him say, "What is it, Button?" and heard a giggle from Selby.

Drew was laughing when he spoke again. "Well, Cathryn, I think I'd better hang up and find out what this little rascal here has done to my shoelaces. Looks like she's tied them together, or am I mistaken?"

Cathryn let out a sigh of relief. "I'll see you soon," she said quickly. Too quickly?

"Day after tomorrow," Drew said. "I can hardly wait."

"I can hardly wait myself," said Cathryn, much too pensively.

Another silence, and then they said good-bye, a bit awkwardly, she thought. When they hung up, there was an emptiness that cried out to be filled.

IN NEW YORK, Drew let his fingers linger on the receiver for a long moment after they'd finished their conversation. Something was wrong. He was sure of it. Those silences...her lack of response at times when, before, he could almost have predicted what she was going to say. She was keeping something from him, he was certain.

He couldn't wait until the day after tomorrow to see her. It was too long. But he and Selby had planned a museum outing today, and Selby had been looking forward to it.

Worried, he consulted the phone directory for the number of the airline on which he and Selby were scheduled to fly back to Palm Beach. Surely they would have an earlier flight he could take. If something were indeed wrong, he would at least know about it, he reasoned, and if not, wouldn't it be terrific to surprise her?

THE NEXT MORNING Judy and Amanda arrived with the good news that Cathryn's Jaguar had been repaired, and in record time, too.

"We stopped by the garage with Daddy before we came here," Amanda announced importantly, "and I could hardly even tell the car had been in an accident."

"Let's make a batch of blueberry pancakes to celebrate," suggested Judy. She produced a container of fresh blueberries from a shopping bag, and they assembled the mixing bowls and ingredients that they would need.

Cathryn was tediously picking over the freshly washed blueberries when the doorbell rang.

Judy, who was helping Amanda measure flour for the batter, looked up in surprise and said, "Are you expecting anyone?"

"No, and Gurney hasn't called." Cathryn knew for a fact that the unreliable intercom was working this morning, because the doorman had used it less than half an hour before to announce Judy and Amanda. There was only one person who had ever managed to get past her doorman, and that was Drew. But she knew better than to expect him today; he wasn't due back in town until tomorrow.

"I'll go," said Judy, leaving the flour to Amanda, who had somehow managed to smudge some on her nose.

Cathryn set the blueberries aside and wiped her damp hands on a towel. She glanced at the clock. It was only nine-thirty, early by Palm Beach standards.

She heard Judy unlatch the door, and she thought, too late, that she should have warned Judy to put the chain on.

Just as she reached the foyer, the door burst open and Cathryn was startled to see Drew, his hair disheveled, his clothes rumpled.

For a moment time hung suspended, the world stopped, and there might have been no one else but the two of them in the room.

"Thank God you're all right," he said before striding across the floor and crushing her in his arms.

Chapter Eleven

Cathryn buried her face against his neck, scarcely daring to believe that it really was Drew. Strong muscles in his arms flexed, convulsed, so that she could barely breathe. The musky male scent of him and the feeling of him pressed close to her dispelled the yearning that had been building up inside her for the past week. She clung to him joyfully, whispering his name over and over, and he raised his hand to frame her face, pulling back so that he could search first her eyes, then her expression.

His gaze took in the gauze bandage on her temple, his hands slid down her arms as though to reassure himself that she was whole. His eyes returned to hers, burning blue and intense.

"You weren't due home until tomorrow," she said shakily. He looked tired; purple half-moons under his eyes told her that he hadn't had much sleep. He hadn't shaved recently, either, and as his mouth met hers, his rough cheek scraped her skin. It felt wonderful.

He kissed her deeply, longingly, and she trembled in his arms as she felt strong stirrings of desire for him. She craved more kisses, more of him, but she was well aware that Judy stood behind her, looking nonplussed. Amanda stared at them, having left the kitchen to investigate the commotion.

Still in a daze, Cathryn broke their embrace for propriety's sake. "Why are you here?" she asked him, hardly able to speak with the happiness of it. She still couldn't believe it.

Drew acted as if he were loath to let her go. He held both her hands in his, gripping them tightly. "I had a funny feeling yesterday after we talked. Something about the way you sounded...."

Cathryn remembered.

"It stayed with me," Drew went on rapidly, "and last night I started calling airlines, trying to hop a flight back. The best I could do was to book an early-bird flight into Palm Beach International, so I grabbed it. And then late last night I remembered I'd promised you to call Susannah while I was in New York. When she told me about your accident, I almost went crazy."

"But Susannah didn't know," Cathryn said in a puzzled tone.

"I told her," said Judy. "I called her yesterday. She'd just arrived back in town after taking a trip to Phoenix with Avery."

"Cathryn, if I hadn't caught a cab from the airport right away, I would have run all the way over here, pulling Selby along with me."

For the first time, Cathryn became conscious of the little girl standing just inside the doorway, self-consciously rubbing one ankle with her other foot and looking even more uncertain than Judy did.

"Come here, Button," said Drew, maintaining his grip on Cathryn's hand and stretching his other hand out to Selby.

Selby didn't want to come at first. She clutched Raggedy Ann in front of her face, peering apprehensively out from behind the red-yarn hair.

"Come on, it's okay." Drew smiled at his daughter. Her anxiety seemed to evaporate as she took a few tentative steps forward.

Instinctively Cathryn knelt down to be on eye level with her.

"Cathryn, this is my daughter, Selby. And Selby, this is my friend, the one who decorated your new room, Cathryn Mulqueen."

Selby regarded Cathryn solemnly. Her eyes shone star-bright; perhaps she had slept on the airplane, because she didn't look the least bit tired. They were blue eyes, like Drew's, but Selby's shaded toward the delicate blue of hyacinths. Like her father's, the blue eyes teamed strikingly with spiked black lashes. Her hair grew as shiny and as black as Drew's, and her skin tone varied from rosy to creamy to translucent. She tipped her heart-shaped face—Talma's face—to one side as she studied Cathryn. Cathryn remembered Talma from her wedding picture at the Hobe Sound house, and one look was enough to tell her that Selby was as much Talma's daughter as she was Drew's.

Cathryn smiled what she hoped was a reassuring smile. "I'm glad to meet you," she said.

When no answer seemed forthcoming, Cathryn stood up and looked to Drew for guidance. But he appeared even more tired than before, and he seemed distracted by Cathryn herself, his eyes worriedly assessing the small bandage on Cathryn's temple.

It was clear to Cathryn that Selby was not going to speak, that she felt overwhelmed by the strangeness of these new people, this apartment she'd never seen before. Cathryn realized that it would be up to her to steer things along a path that all of them would find comfortable.

Forcing herself to think, she said, "Judy, would you mind fixing all of us one of your wonderful breakfasts?" She saw Drew, the confirmed breakfast-hater, start to demur, so she interjected quickly, "I'm sure it's been a long time since Selby has eaten," and she quieted Drew with a significant look.

At this Selby brightened.

"Are you hungry, Button?" asked Drew.

Selby nodded shyly.

Judy stepped forward with a smile. "I'll bet you love pancakes, don't you, Selby?"

Selby nodded again, her eyes darting curiously to Amanda and taking in the light dusting of flour on Amanda's small pug nose.

"I'm mixing some pancake batter," Amanda volunteered. "Maybe you could help."

"I could?" said Selby softly, her eyes sparkling.

"Of course. Come with me into the kitchen and I'll show you," said Judy. "Would you like that?"

Selby nodded. "My mother never lets me into the kitchen."

Judy smiled. "Well, that's one place where I can always use an extra pair of hands." She held out her hand and Selby offered hers trustingly before the three of them marched off to the kitchen.

"Perhaps you'd like to set Raggedy Ann right here in this chair," they heard Judy saying, "and then maybe you'll be ready for a visit to the powder room."

"There's soap that smells like strawberries," confided Amanda gleefully. From the powder room they heard Selby's exclamation of delight, followed by a giggle.

"That smells scrumptious," Selby said in her high clear voice.

Drew looked at Cathryn. Cathryn looked at Drew.

"Judy and Amanda have quite a way with Selby," he said. "I don't know that I've ever seen her take to anyone so quickly."

"Selby is beautiful, Drew," said Cathryn. Really, she'd been impressed with Selby, and not only with her beauty but by the keen intelligence shining from her eyes.

"Yes. And so are you beautiful. Come over here and sit beside me on the couch. Not so far away. There, that's better. Are you really all right? Honestly?" His anxious eyes swept over her.

Cathryn smiled and touched his face gently with her fingertips, tracing the lines, deeper now, around his eyes. She brushed her lips lightly across his cheek, mostly to reassure herself that he was still there.

"I'm fine. Just a few bruises and this cut on my head. I'll be jogging again in a day or so."

"When Susannah told me what had happened to you, I thought I'd go berserk. Things began to add up—those long silences on the phone, your vagueness about your work, the way you often changed the subject for no good reason. How could you do this? You should have told me." He looked momentarily shaken.

"I was afraid you'd worry," she said. "I wanted you to enjoy your time alone with Selby, just as you had planned, without having to trouble yourself about me."

"But you *needed* me. Can you imagine my shock when Susannah told me? I appreciate your unselfishness in allowing me my time with Selby. Only it hurts that you shut me out at a time like this!"

"I—I didn't mean to hurt you, Drew." Her eyes filled with tears, and seeing them, Drew put one hand to the back of her head and pulled her forehead to his shoulder.

"Sh, it's all right," he comforted.

"You do understand?"

"Of course I do. But when were you going to tell me?"

She lifted her head, met his eyes. "I thought that when you came back, we'd talk on the phone and I could explain. I had no idea you'd come bursting in here unannounced. Although," she hastened to add, curving into the arm he slid around her, "I'm delighted that you did. Oh, Drew, I've missed you terribly.''

He nuzzled at her throat, exhaling. "I missed you, too."

Her mouth went suddenly dry with her joy at having him so near.

"What I missed most was holding you in my arms, feeling our hearts beating together," he whispered. "Just the way we are now."

"I was so lonely for you," she admitted. "Everything hurt after the accident, and I wanted you more than anything."

"I wish I could have been here for you," he said before capturing her lips in a deep and caring kiss that made up for all the pain and longing she'd suffered. He released her lips to murmur, "Oh, Cathryn, I love you. So much. You have no idea."

"I do so," she said, her whisper like a sigh before her lips found his.

In the kitchen Selby chortled over something, and above the child's high voice she heard Judy's lower one, with Amanda chiming in at intervals. Drew cradled Cathryn in his arms, kissed her hair above the bandage, held her close. These moments alone were theirs and no one else's—not Judy's, not Amanda's and not Selby's.

"Breakfast is ready!" cried an excited Selby from the kitchen. "I flipped the pancakes myself!"

Drew groaned, a groan that only Cathryn could hear. "And *this* gives me another reason to hate breakfast," he whispered, making Cathryn's mouth curve upward against his.

"Wait until you taste Judy's pancakes," she said, grinning up at him. "They're strictly out of the ordinary."

"I'd rather taste you," he said, his eyes traveling to the vee of her robe where her breasts swelled gently and provocatively. "I can't wait until you give me a proper welcome."

She pulled her robe tighter around her; their mouths joined fleetingly, and Cathryn called out to the kitchen contingent, "We're on our way."

And so the proper welcome had to wait.

Breakfast was made delightful by the chattering interplay between the two little girls. Then Judy and Amanda said their good-byes, after many promises between Selby and Amanda to see each other soon.

Drew was so exhausted at this point that as much as Cathryn wanted him with her, as much as she would have liked to get to know the winsome sprite named Selby, who kept shooting curious, covert glances in her direction, she urged them both to go home and take a nap.

"I'm not tired," Drew protested over and over, but Cathryn didn't believe him.

Finally he and Selby left and Cathryn was alone again, but she told herself that she really didn't mind, she needed to work anyway, and there would be plenty of time for them to spend together later.

For his part, Drew was grateful for Cathryn's understanding. He returned to his Palm Beach apartment, so recently and so lovingly redecorated with his and his daughter's tastes in mind. He introduced an awed Selby to her new room, saw her settled in for a nap, and then fell across his own king-sized bed and slept for hours, worn out with worry over Cathryn.

THE NEXT MORNING Cathryn pulled on her pink-velour warm-up suit and jogged across the street to the beach for the first time since her accident, not knowing for sure if she would see Drew or not. But there he was, swimming along the swell of a wave, and the tiny figure sitting on the sand watching him was Selby.

She ran toward them, her heart so buoyant that she might have been flying. Physically, she felt wonderful, the best she'd felt since the accident, almost as good as new. She slowed her run to a walk as she approached Selby.

"Hi," said Cathryn easily.

Selby looked up, puzzled at first and clearly not expecting to see anyone she knew. Then she smiled, pure sunshine. "Hi," she replied, recognizing Cathryn. "I didn't know you'd be here."

"I like to run on the beach every morning," said Cathryn, easing herself down on the sand beside the child. Selby was so small, smaller than she'd expected, and her movements were delicate and graceful. She searched for signs of Drew in his child. He was there in her black hair and blue eyes, and there was something of him in the set of Selby's small chin. Warmth and a desire to know, *really* know, Selby moved her so much that she wanted to reach out and draw this child, this part of Drew, close to her. But, of course, she didn't. It was too early for that. Better to take it slow and easy for now.

"I like the way you fixed up my room," said Selby, not at all shy now. "It's so pretty."

"I'm glad you like it," Cathryn replied.

"My daddy likes to swim," Selby told her, gesturing toward Drew out in the ocean.

"I know. Do you?"

"Oh, yes. Lots."

"Aren't you going to swim this morning?" Cathryn asked. Selby's swimsuit wasn't wet.

"Yes, when Daddy says it's okay. He's swimming laps. See him turn around and swim the other way?" From out in the water, Drew waved before setting out in the other direction.

Selby ran her eyes over Cathryn curiously, and this made Cathryn feel oddly uncomfortable. "Have you known my father long?"

"A few months," Cathryn replied. Under the little girl's frankly appraising stare, she began to grow fidgety.

"Hello, there," called Drew, who had finished his laps and was splashing toward them through the shallow waves that curled over themselves one after the other toward shore. Selby's eyes flew to Drew, sparkling with joy. She stood up and bounced up and down in excitement.

Selby loves her father, thought Cathryn. This didn't surprise her, but her reaction to that love, so clearly reciprocated in Drew's adoring expression, did. There was something beautiful about that kind of father-daughter interaction, something touching in their delight at being together.

In the past months she had learned to feel and experience many facets of love with Drew. But this was a different kind of love, the love between parent and child, and for some reason seeing it now between Drew and Selby was strangely moving.

Drew stood with his arm around Selby's slight shoulders, and she slid her arm around his waist. They faced Cathryn in the early-morning sunlight, smiles on their faces, a family unit.

"I hope you wore your swimsuit," Drew said to Cathryn. "We're going to swim for a while, and we'd love to have you join us." He spoke sincerely. He wanted her to know that she was welcome.

Cathryn shook her head, feeling very much an outsider in spite of Drew's obvious effort to include her.

"I'm afraid I didn't come prepared to swim," she said, and she wondered with dismay why she sounded so prim and proper, like the old Cathryn, as though she were trying to put distance between herself and the two of them. It was that old habit of hers, no doubt, the cool distancing when confronted with a difficult situation.

Drew's gaze penetrated her; it told her silently that he loved her. He knew what she was thinking and feeling.

"Come on, Daddy," urged Selby, removing her arm from his waist to tug at his hand. "I want you to ride me on your shoulders in the water."

"In a minute," he said, his eyes leaving Cathryn's face and resting upon Selby's.

Selby turned and raced into the gently rising waves, laughing as one broke against her stomach and unexpectedly splashed salt water in her face.

"Wait for me," he cautioned Selby. Then he turned and smiled ruefully at Cathryn. "Guess I'm in the business of providing seashore rides—for the moment, anyway." He kept turning his eyes toward Selby, who squealed with glee as every little wave rode by and threatened to sweep her off her feet.

"And later?"

"Daddy!" Selby was getting out a little too deep, and Drew's eyes flashed anxiously toward her.

"Whoa! I'll be there in a second!" he called. And to Cathryn he said, "I'll have to let you know when we can see each other." His eyes apologized in the split second that they rested on her, but his real attention was all on his daughter.

Cathryn watched as Drew dived into the waves and, swimming underwater, reached Selby and swam between her legs, standing up as she clung happily to his head. Their happiness in being together was very evident, and Cathryn could not, would not, feel jealous. Instead, she made a concentrated effort to enjoy vicariously Drew's pleasure as he cavorted with his daughter.

But their joy was not hers and she felt excluded; she walked thoughtfully back to the apartment building, wondering bleakly how—or perhaps *if*—she and Drew were going to manage any kind of relationship, meaningful or otherwise, now that he seemed only to have eyes for his daughter.

A FEW DAYS LATER, Cathryn and Judy sheltered from the brilliant June sunlight on a park bench beneath a giant ficus tree, watching Amanda as she played in the park. The three of them had spent the morning together, eaten Cathryn's special spinach quiche for lunch, and strolled to the park so that Amanda could play while the two adults visited.

"You seem so preoccupied today," Judy said, looking at her friend critically. She couldn't tell whether Cathryn's peaked look was a lingering effect of her accident or a symptom of something else.

"Do I?" Cathryn abstractedly watched Amanda as she flew off the end of the slide with an excited whoop and ran around to clamber up the steps for another turn.

"Yes, you do. What's wrong, Cathryn? Aren't things going well with Drew and Selby?"

Leave it to Judy to cut right to the middle of it, thought Cathryn. "Everything is fine," she insisted.

Cathryn knew right away that her words hadn't rung true.

"You're not convincing me," Judy replied, with a knowing look.

"Well, everything is almost fine," amended Cathryn, staring unhappily down at her hands to avoid Judy's sharp eyes.

"What is *that* supposed to mean?"

"It's wonderful to have Drew home. I'm getting to know Selby, and I like her a lot."

"But?"

"But Drew and I haven't been alone since they returned from New York. Everywhere we go, Selby goes, too. He lets her stay up to watch the late television movie every night, just so that he can spend more time with her. He even takes her to the office for the little time he spends there these days so that the two of them won't lose any time together. It doesn't leave any time for the two of us."

Judy kept a watchful eye on Amanda as she stumbled and fell. Amanda picked herself up and ran away, laughing. Judy returned her attention to Cathryn. "Doesn't he know any baby-sitters?"

"I guess not. I mean, I don't know. All I know is that I want him and I miss him, and I wish we didn't always have a seven-year-old in tow. I know it sounds selfish and petty and—" She gulped. She couldn't go on.

"You miss doing the things you and Drew used to do together."

"Yes," said Cathryn miserably. She thought of the long candlelight dinners on her balcony, of the languid lovemaking that always followed. Selby's constant presence had put an end to those pleasant interludes. With a sharp stab of guilt, Cathryn quickly pulled herself back from such unworthy thoughts. She was happy that Drew had his daughter with him, wasn't she?

Judy rested her lightly freckled hand on that of her friend. "I'd say such feelings are normal in a case like this," she said reassuringly. Amanda flew by, and Judy's eyes followed her daughter.

Cathryn nodded, not minding that her friend's attention was automatically divided between her and Amanda as Judy in her role as mother watched protectively over her child at play.

And then it was as though a light bulb went on inside Cathryn's head, illuminating a previously obscure truth. Judy was no less a friend because she was a mother. The relationship between Cathryn and Judy had of necessity rearranged itself when Amanda was born, but their longtime friendship had not been diminished, only changed.

This thought gave Cathryn pause, and she ran it through her mind once again. It was something to think about as she became integrated into a threesome composed of Drew, Selby and herself. It was what she wanted with Drew, too. She didn't want to be selfish and petty. She wanted a relationship with Drew that was not diminished by Selby's presence, only different, maybe even enhanced. The idea gave her a new outlook and something to strive toward, and her spirits began to lift at the prospect.

"You know what?" said Judy with a sly look. "It has suddenly occurred to me that there's a solution to this problem."

Cathryn blinked. "What?" she said.

"Trust me," Judy answered, smiling enigmatically.

THE NEXT EVENING Cathryn had just returned to her penthouse after another hectic day at the studio when the phone began to ring. Ordinarily she would have let her answering service pick up the call, but this time, for some reason, she ran to answer it.

"Thank goodness it's you, Cathryn," said Drew's voice in relief. "I'm so tired of getting your answering service!"

"I just walked in the door," she said, sitting down on the edge of her desk, surprised that it was Drew. He never called at this time of day anymore; he was usually preparing dinner for Selby and himself.

"Well, get ready to walk out the door again. With me."

"With you and Selby?"

"No, with me. Aren't I enough?" She could tell from his voice that his eyes must be sparkling devilishly as he spoke to her.

"Where's Selby?"

"Invited to spend the night with Amanda, and she jumped at the chance. Remind me to do something nice for Judy sometime."

Judy. Bless her. This meant that Cathryn and Drew would have a long, uninterrupted time together—in fact, the whole night.

"Where are we going?" she asked him.

"Does it matter? Wherever we're going, we're going together."

Drew sounded as lighthearted as she felt.

"I'll be ready in fifteen minutes," she said, smiling into the phone.

"Make that ten. Or better yet, five. See you soon."

THEY DROVE TO A SEAFOOD RESTAURANT at Jupiter Inlet where they sat on the open-air deck beneath the stars and the slowly revolving beam of the old red lighthouse. Afterward Drew drove slowly to Hobe Sound, keeping his arm around her all the way.

"Let's go for a walk on the beach," she said impulsively as they drove up in front of Drew's house. It felt so wonderful to be alone with him again; she wanted to savor every moment, capture every memory, and create more memories to unfold later.

He dug a blanket out of the car trunk and tossed it around his neck before they walked around the house; its cedar-shake roof looked silvered in the moonlight.

The moon unfurled a ribbon of misty light on the billowing sea. Deserted dunes lay shadowed and quiet, and the grass growing there bent only slightly in the sea breeze. The familiar tang of salt air filled Cathryn's nostrils, and the fragrance exhilarated her.

Just being with Cathryn again filled Drew with happiness. "Let's run," he said, taking her hand, and they raced side by side along the hard, wet sand, holding hands tightly, until Cathryn slowed down, gasping.

"That was a good performance for a nonjogger," she told him.

"Yes, but I'm out of breath," he said. "I'll spread the blanket and we can sit here for a while." They found a level place above the high-tide line, and she helped Drew settle the blanket, tucking each corner under a little pocket of sand so that the breeze wouldn't disturb it. They sat down and Drew slipped an arm around her shoulders, bringing her close.

Neither of them spoke for a while; they simply watched the race of waves approaching the shore.

"I've almost forgotten what it was like to be alone with you," said Drew finally.

"Yes," she said.

"It's not that I haven't wanted to be," he replied.

"I know."

He kissed her gently on the forehead, just below the almost invisible scar from her accident. "You know, it's not easy being a single father. I never thought I'd be one, you see, and I'm totally unprepared."

"What's the hardest part about it?"

"Not being able to see you as often as I'd like," he said without hesitation. "I keep thinking that I've only got a matter of weeks with Selby, and then she'll go back to Talma. Several weeks out of the year, Cathryn. There are countless other weeks when I won't be able to watch her making faces at the puppies in the pet store or listening to me read her a story or concentrating hard when she draws a picture for me. I want to enjoy everything about our time together that I can."

"I understand, Drew. It's hard having to share you, though, after having you all to myself."

His eyes softened to dark-blue velvet. "But you like Selby, don't you?"

"I think she's wonderful. She's spontaneous, cheerful, outgoing and altogether very dear." She paused, wishing she knew a tactful way to put what she wanted to say into words without hurting his feelings. "I'm very fond of Selby. But I can't deny that having her here has put a strain on our relationship. You know, one time you said, right here on this beach, that it's just the two of us, even in a crowd of people?"

He nodded, remembering the occasion well. It had been when he had suggested that she might be lonely with just the two of them, had thought she might want to ask Amanda and Judy to the Hobe Sound house so she'd have some company. He'd been touched to learn that Cathryn found everything she needed in his presence, even when he was too busy to pay much attention to her.

"Well," she went on, drawing the courage to speak from his understanding expression, "these days, sometimes I feel that three's a crowd. I don't feel that it's just you and me anymore. And it hurts." There, for better or worse, she'd said it. She hoped he wouldn't misconstrue her honest expression of her feelings as criticism of Selby.

He regarded her cautiously, perplexed. "But it is just the two of us," he said in surprise. "You and me together, with the addition of Selby." He was hurt. She could tell by the way his arm stiffened around her shoulders.

"If that's true, if it really is still you and me, you'll have to make more time for us," she said, and her voice broke with the tension of it.

In a rush of intense empathy, of understanding the way things seemed from her point of view, he drew her gently into his arms, feeling the warmth of her body, the sweet miracle of her. He had never meant to hurt her, but he had been torn between Cathryn and his daughter. Now he saw that he had slighted Cathryn in his eagerness to resume his relationship with his daughter, and it was clear to him that if he wanted to keep Cathryn, things would have to change.

The truth of it was that he had been without her too long. "My dear Cat," he murmured, "I will make time for us. It won't be easy, but now that I know you feel so strongly about it, we'll manage. We'll work it out, I promise."

Cathryn turned her head to reveal the unabashed desire in her eyes. Drew bent his head until his lips found hers, and their kiss was long and sweet, increasing in passion. His hands trembled as he touched her, not merely touching her but discovering her all over again. He wanted to rediscover all of her, to renew his sensation of her full, upturned breasts, to let his hands roam downward to the smooth, round fullness of her hips, to explore the most intimate places.

Beneath his hands she seemed familiar but somehow different after so long a time. Had her ear always been so neatly curved, so flat and perfect, swirled like a seashell? Were her fingers always so long and tapered, and had they ever before caressed him so elegantly?

One of Drew's hands wove itself into her hair as he eased her head back until her throat arched, the most sensitive skin now exposed for his kisses.

His mouth on her burning skin sent heat waves radiating through her body, and she moaned in readiness. This was what she had wanted for so long; it was what she had been waiting for. His hand released her hair and glided to the zipper at the back of her dress. Very slowly, he skimmed the zipper down and parted the fabric. He unhooked the wisp of silk that held her breasts and slipped the dress off her shoulders. At the same time she worked at the buttons of his shirt so that he could shrug it off and loosened his pants until he was able to slide out of them in one fluid movement. His hands stroked her sides, then curled around to support her breasts, white in the moonlight, while he admired them almost reverently.

Then she was lying back on the blanket, arms reaching up for him in silent entreaty. He paused for a moment to marvel at the beauty of her as she lay before him in the moonlight, her hair spilling across the sand in blue-white splendor, her lips moist and slightly parted. He thought she had never looked more beautiful and he had never wanted her more than he did at that instant.

"I love you," he told her unsteadily, gathering her to him.

"I love you," she whispered, feeling the true emotion of her words.

Cathryn trailed a string of kisses from his mouth downward until she had to roll him over to his back so that her lips and tongue could work their magic down his body, across his stomach, along his thighs.

"Cathryn," he said, and the name was a moan. She was making him wait for what he wanted most, and the wait was wonderful agony.

When he was so desperate for her that he could no longer stand the anguish, he sat up and lifted her face so that he could see his adoration of her reflected back to him in her rapturous expression. She shone naked and pale and white in the light from the moon, and her hair tumbled over his thighs like a froth of moonbeams.

He would have liked to be gentler with her after so long a time; he wanted to cherish her and savor the delight. But the need was strong within him, and he could wait no longer. He clasped her to him, fusing his mouth to hers. And she returned his ardor measure for measure, turning on her back, pulling him along with her.

Lowering himself over her, face to face, her long body pressed tightly beneath his, he clutched her to him as they melded together for moments before exploding in a starburst of bright light.

The power behind the act was enough to make her gasp and then moan with her own explosion, a white-hot fusion that melted the ice within her.

They lay locked in each other's arms, shaken by the release of so much feeling; tears stung Cathryn's eyes. Their intimacy had been revived, their relationship revitalized. Again they felt the encompassing closeness that had made the two of them together so very special, almost from the beginning.

Drew held her close, wondering how he could have been so wrong. He had tried to exorcise the last lingering pain of his past life by clinging to his child as though she were the last life preserver from a ship that had sunk. But she wasn't enough to keep him afloat. He needed this woman, Cathryn. She was part of the life he could live from now on, and that was what really counted, not the life he had left behind.

When he could speak, he said, "I never want to be without you again. Never. Marry me, Cathryn." And as he kissed her eyes, still bright with the joyful tears, her heart stilled and grew solemn with the thought of it.

Marriage, she thought, awestruck by the idea. *Marriage.* Although she loved Drew with all her heart, Cathryn couldn't be sure: was marriage the kind of union she'd been searching for?

Chapter Twelve

"Hold still—that's right. Just let me dab on a bit more highlighter," said Cathryn, scrutinizing Selby's face through narrowed eyes. Selby stood gazing at herself in Cathryn's mirror with unconcealed delight.

The idea of a complete makeup job just for fun had been Selby's idea, and Cathryn had been pleased to oblige. Together they had rummaged through Cathryn's makeup drawer, searching for just the right shade of eyeliner to emphasize Selby's blue eyes and exactly the right shade of lipstick to complement her fair skin.

"How's it going?" asked Drew, poking his head around the edge of the bathroom door. Selby closed her eyes to show off the elaborate layers of eyeshadow.

"What do you think?" said Cathryn critically, surveying her work.

"I think I have a very pretty little girl who is going to grow up to be a very beautiful big girl," he said, scarcely able to take his eyes off Selby. "And when do we eat dinner? It's ready."

"Right now, if you like," said Cathryn.

"I like. Anyway, what kind of a deal is this? You invite us over to eat pompano en papillote, and then you snatch my daughter out from under my very eyes and disappear, and I have to put the finishing touches on the meal. Some hostess you are."

"You have to learn to be a little impulsive once in a while," she informed him.

Selby, who was turning this way and that as she examined her reflection, grinned up at her. "Thank you, Cathryn," she said, hugging Cathryn around the waist. "Is it okay if I leave all this makeup on?"

"If your father doesn't mind," she said.

"Daddy?"

"Okay, Button. I've learned to be impulsive." He kissed Cathryn surreptitiously as Selby preceded them to the balcony where Cathryn had set the table for dinner.

This is what it would be like if Drew and I were married, Cathryn thought as she deftly poured the Chablis. She had told him she'd have to think about it, that she didn't want either of them to rush into something as serious as marriage. Now, the three of them gathered around the table together gave Cathryn a cozy, belonging feeling, an impression of family life that she had never shared with anyone before. Selby sat across from her, looking so grown-up in her adult makeup. Cathryn felt a tug at her heartstrings over this child who was not her child, yet had grown so dear to her. It was a fondness that surpassed her obligation to be nice to Selby because she was Drew's daughter. She had truly grown to care for Selby in a very special way.

True to his word, Drew had made time for her in his life and Selby's since that night on the beach. And there had been time for her to be alone with Drew, too. Even though they had not discussed it further, marriage had weighed heavily on their minds. There were so many factors involved, factors that weren't usually involved in the decisions of ordinary people. Drew had his work with Sedgwick Department Stores; Cathryn had the demands of her career. And, of course, there was Selby.

Cathryn knew, because he had said so, that Drew was pleased that she and Selby had grown so close. Cathryn had learned Selby's weaknesses and strengths and limits. She'd become open and receptive to Selby's needs. Drew had watched and had encouraged the bond between them to strengthen and grow.

"Let's all go on a picnic together," he'd suggest, or he'd say, "Cathryn, do you think Selby needs another swimsuit, or does she have enough?" Involving her in decisions concerning his daughter was his way of involving her ever more deeply in his life.

It was an involvement that Cathryn wanted. She longed to be close to Drew, part of Drew, in every way. But marriage? She thought about it all the time, when she was with him and as she worked. Eventually she'd have to deal with it, she knew, but for now she was putting it off, making it wait while she played for time.

Cathryn had finally finished work on the architect's office, and he'd been so pleased that he had given a grand reception to show off the results of her work. Mrs. Brattigan's green house was now redecorated in shades of yellow, and she had happily pronounced the new color scheme delightful before flying off to Newport.

But Cathryn was busy now with other projects, and so, knowing how preoccupied she was, Drew had refrained from bringing up the subject of marriage again. He wanted to approach the idea gently, carefully, to avoid scaring her away.

She'd looked so stunned when he'd asked her to marry him, although he knew she had probably thought about it. He'd certainly thought about it often enough: the pleasure of waking up beside her every morning, the beatific smile on her face as she snuggled into his arms for a moment of closeness before they began their separate days. He'd daydreamed about marriage, fantasized, and pulled himself back from the precipice of actually asking her hundreds of times before he'd finally proposed. His hesitation didn't signify reluctance. He simply knew that he couldn't think about marriage to her until he knew how she got along with Selby.

His daughter was the single most important responsibility in his life. Her welfare was his primary concern, and custody of Selby seemed more important all the time. He had seen, since she had been living with him, that Selby was an emotionally stable child and could probably handle a custody battle between her parents. Cathryn would be a wonderful stepmother, if only she knew it.

Drew hadn't believed how easily the relationship between Selby and Cathryn had flourished. He should have realized that Cathryn had a way with children when he'd seen her with Amanda. But he hadn't known how well she would get along with his daughter until he'd actually observed it. And it was then that he'd known he wanted to marry Cathryn, wanted it more than anything in the world.

After dinner, when they were sitting on the balcony watching a half-moon rise over the darkening sea, Cathryn said suddenly, "Have you heard from Talma lately?" Selby had gone to thumb through a stack of Cathryn's magazines, leaving them in privacy.

Drew sent her a surprised glance. "Selby's had a postcard from her mother. Talma is in Rome, and she doesn't know when she's coming back. Why do you ask?"

Cathryn shrugged. "Just interested. Selby doesn't mention her mother very often."

Drew was silent for a long time. "She's beginning to open up about life with her mother. Frankly, Cathryn, it disturbs me. Talma's a nervous, anxious woman—she has wild temper tantrums, and I'm sure Selby often feels frightened. Selby seemed so tense the first few days we were together in New York; she's relaxed and adjusted now. The other day she said she wished she could live with me instead of Talma. I'm beginning to think more and more about getting custody of her. What do you think?"

"I've only seen Selby here, of course, but there's no doubt in my mind that she's a happy child when she's with you."

"Talma isn't easy to deal with. We're barely on speaking terms. If I go for custody of my daughter and fail to get it, Talma could create chaos every time I wanted to see Selby. I want to do what's best for Selby." A line furrowed its way across Drew's forehead.

"What about counseling? It might help Talma."

Drew shook his head. "She's been seeing a psychiatrist for years. We saw a marriage counselor before we split. No, I'm sure that's not the answer."

"Then," Cathryn said quietly, "you must do what you think best."

What Drew thought best was to marry Cathryn. The three of them would be a family. There was nothing he wanted more.

Did she want that, too? Sometimes he saw the warm light in her green-and-gold eyes when she looked at Selby, or when she laughed with her, and there was a lot of laughter between Cathryn and his daughter. Tonight during dinner he could have sworn she was thinking about how it would be if the three of them gathered around a dinner table at the end of each and every day. Why wouldn't she say she'd marry him? She loved him. He was sure of that.

She also loved her work. He understood how dedicated she was to her studio. And he was proud of what she had done. Being married to him would preclude such a busy working schedule, he knew, and that would be good for Cathryn. He wanted to persuade her to slow down, to take it easy for a while, just as Judy had been after her to do for so long. His own work schedule had been drastically altered since Selby arrived, and he felt much better as a result, both mentally and physically. He'd hoped that Selby's presence would promote a slacking off in Cathryn's own determination to work so hard. And now, the perfect opportunity had presented itself, a chance for Cathryn to find out for herself how good it would be to have Selby around for longer than an hour or two at one time.

He cleared his throat. "I have a favor to ask of you, sweetheart," he said. He watched her carefully; behind his casual manner, he was alert for danger signals.

She reached over and pressed her hand on his, absently stroking his fingers. "Anything," she said, with a look that was mellow and full of contentment.

Drew relaxed, felt relieved at her easy response. *This,* he thought, *is what it would be like if we were married. Every night, knowing each other, being best friends, contented.*

"The construction outfit that's building our new Daytona Beach store is having problems. Yesterday the roof collapsed, and now there's some question about how it's to be repaired. I have to go to Daytona tomorrow morning, and I need someone to look after Selby. You know a construction site is no place for a small girl. Can she stay with you for a night or two?"

With a sinking feeling, Cathryn thought of her new projects. Her assistant, Zohra, had been out sick for the past week; Cathryn had taken over handling the details for Zohra's clients. It wasn't a good time to take on a baby-sitting job, even with as sweet a child as Selby.

But in her eagerness to please Drew, Cathryn didn't hesitate. Somehow she would manage. She smiled and said, "Of course. I'd like having Selby stay with me."

"I could ask Judy, but we've accepted so much of her hospitality already," he said, giving Cathryn an out if she chose to take it.

"No," Cathryn said firmly. "I want Selby here." She entwined her fingers in his.

He squeezed her hand, thinking how pretty her hair looked at night with the light from the room behind them shining on it. He felt a glow of pleasure at her willingness to accommodate his needs.

"I'll bring Selby over early tomorrow morning so that I can get on the road," he told her. Cathryn lowered her head, just in time to hide her look of sudden apprehension.

IT WOULD HAVE BEEN EASIER if Drew had been gone only a short time, as he had originally planned. But on the second day he called from Daytona to tell Cathryn and Selby with some exasperation that nothing was going as expected and that he'd have to spend the whole week there.

Selby was delighted. Cathryn, much as she tried not to be, was dismayed.

What a lot of fun the two of them had had for the first two days! Cathryn had called her studio and asked Renee to take on Zohra's work, and Renee had politely agreed. Cathryn didn't go to the studio at all. Instead, she took Selby to Woolworth's and bought her not just one parakeet but two. Selby named them Romeo and Juliet after two other famous lovebirds, and they watched entranced as the birds billed and cooed at each other and at the mirror hanging in their cage.

On the second day they curled Selby's hair with Cathryn's hot rollers and then, dissatisfied with the look of it, combed all the curls out. They read *Peter Pan* to each other. And they cooked a batch of fudge that never hardened, so that they'd had to scoop it out of the pan with a spoon. Cathryn pulled out her old watercolors and taught Selby a bit about painting. She even started a painting of her own, done from memory, of the spreading oak tree overlooking the dunes at the Hobe Sound house. She was amazed at how much she enjoyed working with watercolors again.

"I really need to go into the studio today," Cathryn told Selby firmly on the third day after Drew had called and said that he wasn't coming home as scheduled. She planned to ask Judy if Selby could go over and visit Amanda.

"Can I go along to the studio?" asked Selby unexpectadly.

"Well," said Cathryn, but then she thought, *Why not? It would be interesting for Selby.* And so she took her to the studio and handed her a pencil and some paper. Selby sat patiently beside Rita for the first several hours, asking questions, playing with the stapler and drawing pictures. Then she became restless, fidgeting until Rita responded by taking her to a nearby ice-cream parlor. When Rita went home at five, Selby wanted Cathryn to leave, too.

"I can't, Selby," insisted Cathryn, running her hand nervously through her hair while answering yet another phone call.

Selby retreated to Rita's desk, where she managed to amuse herself with the typewriter for the better part of an hour, and Selby's reproachful look when Cathryn managed to wind things up made Cathryn feel rotten.

Cathryn described one of the interiors she was designing to Selby that night over grilled-cheese-and-bacon sandwiches, and rather desperately asked her for suggestions. But Selby's suggestions weren't usable, and afterward Cathryn sat at her drafting table staring glumly at a set of house plans, wondering how she was going to manage if Drew didn't show up soon.

"I love you," Drew said when he called every night, but suddenly and inexplicably that wasn't enough anymore. She decided that she wouldn't feel comfortable telling him that she couldn't work, especially since the reason she couldn't work was the presence of his daughter. Each time she hung up the phone after speaking with him, she felt more depressed than before.

One night out of pure exasperation she convinced Selby to go to bed early, hoping to work on a design plan for a new high-rise office building in West Palm Beach. But she was so tired from the day's activities,

which had included chasing the two escaped para-
keets around the apartment and then cleaning up their
droppings, that she couldn't think, much less create.

"Are you getting tired of having me here?" asked
Selby the next day when Cathryn was distractedly
folding one of the many towels that had proliferated
alarmingly since the child had arrived in the
apartment.

Her eyes met Selby's, which were full of a need for
reassurance. She dropped the towels and gathered
Selby into her arms, wondering how she could love a
child so much yet long so desperately for some time of
her own.

She called Judy for relief, and Judy immediately
offered to take Selby home to play with Amanda for
an afternoon.

"Wonderful," breathed Cathryn. That day she sat
down, and feeling uninhibited for the first time since
Selby's arrival, she zipped through three of her assistants' design plans and with a sigh of relief marked
them with her approval.

WHEN DREW RETURNED from Daytona at the end of
the week, he found a harried and exhausted Cathryn.

His heart sank. He hadn't expected this. He had
been so sure that everything would go well, that both
Cathryn and Selby would thrive on full-time togeth-
erness. It hadn't been his fault that he'd had to stay in
Daytona longer than planned.

"Tell me what's wrong," he insisted, expecting Cathryn to pour out her feelings, so that he could soothe away her insecurities.

She couldn't tell him that having Selby around had made it difficult for her to work. "It's the new office building," she lied, remembering when she'd found it so difficult to lie to him. When you loved someone, was it always difficult to lie? Did it get easier, or did the act of lying imply a loss of love? She tried to forget these concerns in their lovemaking after Selby had gone to bed.

But this time her passion was muted, and she drew no peace from Drew's body. Her own body was left tense.

Afterward Drew said quietly, holding her close, listening to her even breathing, "It wasn't good for you, was it?"

When she didn't reply, pretending to be asleep, he knew that it hadn't been, and he felt a sharp stab of despair and remorse. He shouldn't have left Selby with her so long; it had been a mistake. He should have acquainted Cathryn with full-time caretaking duties more slowly, as he had planned to do in the first place. But he had thought it would be all right. And it wasn't.

HE CALLED CATHRYN the next night, wanting to see her.

"I can't tonight," she said, her voice sounding curiously remote, almost as it had the first time he'd met her, when she'd withdrawn completely.

"You're still planning on that sales leaders' banquet with me tomorrow night, aren't you?" It was the biggest event of the year for the sales leaders in the Sedgwick Department Stores empire; every summer Drew hosted a dinner dance for them at the Breakers, and he'd been looking forward to attending this one with Cathryn on his arm.

For a moment she didn't speak, and then she said, "I don't think so, Drew. The new office building..." Her voice trailed off into thin air. "Please forgive me. I have so much work to do."

A numbing coldness swept over him after saying good-bye, and he hung up feeling desolate. He now knew without a doubt that she was deliberately avoiding him.

Cathryn sat beside her telephone, tears streaming down her face. She hadn't wanted to hurt him; she loved him.

But at the moment she needed space, and time away from him and Selby. She had to think about what marriage and the stepmothering of a little girl would mean to her career and to her life.

"WHAT'S WRONG WITH MARRIAGE?" asked Judy when Cathryn confided her fears. "I think you and Drew would be very happy."

"You know my work has always come first," replied Cathryn unhappily. "I love Drew, but I've got so many new contracts. Ever since I've been seeing Drew, my work has suffered. I was four weeks behind schedule on the architect's office, and if he hadn't been understanding, he could have done my business a good deal of damage.''

"Is that all you think about? Even now that you have Drew and Selby?''

"It's not all I think about, no," insisted Cathryn. "But I'm used to thinking about such things first. Everything else always came after my work.''

"Even people?''

"Even people. Well, most people, anyway. But when I have more time—''

"When you have more time, I hope Drew is still available," said Judy tartly. Seeing the crestfallen expression on Cathryn's face, she sighed and said, "So when do you get some free time?''

"Soon, I hope—in a month or so, the first week in October when I go to New York for that conference, the one where I'm going to be the banquet speaker.'' That was another thing—the speech she had to make. She'd committed herself to it last year, before she'd even met Drew. Giving the speech was the last thing she wanted to do, but the League of Interior Designers was counting on her and she had turned them down last year. She was an award-winning designer, and she had an obligation; she couldn't bow out again, not at the last minute, anyway.

"Cathryn, make time to spend with Drew. He made time to spend with you when you needed it.''

This pointed reference to Drew's understanding of her needs only made Cathryn feel worse. Drew had comprehended exactly how she felt when he'd shut her out. Now she was shutting him out, rejecting him, and she hated herself for it.

But it was different now. When Drew had first entered her life, he had been a well from which she could replenish her energy. He had sparked creativity in her in some strange, inexplicable way. But now that their lives were both arranged around a child, she was distracted and tired.

Cathryn sensed that both Judy and Drew thought she was being selfish, was dooming their chances by being adamant about maintaining the same level of involvement in her work. And she couldn't shake the conviction that if they couldn't work things out it would be her fault. The guilt trip was staggering.

"I don't know what to do," she said bleakly, feeling torn.

"Some things are more important than work and money," said Judy sagely.

Cathryn didn't reply. It seemed to her that if she married Drew and gave herself over to him and to Selby, she would be losing the very thing, her work, that made her who she was.

Judy, dedicated wife and mother, would never understand. The only person Cathryn could expect to understand was Drew, and he was part of the problem.

"CATHRYN, COME WITH SELBY AND ME out in the canoe." Drew and Selby had showed up unannounced at the studio after five o'clock in the evening when everyone but Cathryn had gone home; daylight saving time gave them more hours of light.

She tried to smile. "I can't, Drew," she said carefully. "I have too much work to do."

"Please, Cathryn," chimed in Selby. "I can't paddle hard enough to make any difference. Daddy wants to go all the way up the coast of Lake Worth to Palm Beach Inlet. If you don't go, we'll only be able to go as far as the bridge."

"I wish I could, Selby," she said, hardening her heart to Selby's persuasion, "but I'm waiting for an important phone call."

"Oh." Selby's face fell in disappointment.

"Let me talk with Cathryn alone, Button," Drew said gently.

"Okay." Selby whirled and skipped down the darkened hallway, peering curiously into the room where upholstery samples were kept.

"Cathryn, I had hoped—"

"Drew, I'm sorry. I really am. I know you've been successful in arranging your working hours around spending time with Selby, and I'm glad. I understand that it's what you want, what you've always planned to do if she were here. But don't you see, I can't do that. I have other demands on my time, other important things to do." She gestured impatiently at the papers on her desk.

"The fresh air and exercise would do you good," he said quietly, his eyes exploring her face as though it were entirely new territory, a land uncharted.

"I wish I could go," she said unhappily. "But I can't."

Drew lifted his hands helplessly, then let them fall. "All right," he said. "All right."

She watched Drew walk down the hall, listened to him call to Selby.

"'Bye, Cathryn," called Selby before the door closed behind them, leaving the studio silent except for Cathryn's long sigh.

This had happened before more than once, Drew and Selby expecting her to drop everything to do something with them. Instead of feeling pleased at being included in their plans, Cathryn could only feel deep irritation at their wanting her to conform to their schedule. Wasn't Drew using Selby's adorable presence to manipulate her? Or was he just trying to share himself and his daughter with her? Cathryn could see it both ways, but from either perpective, she felt conflict.

She had thought that having curtailed her time spent with Drew, she'd be able to work steadily again. It hadn't turned out that way. She'd sit at her desk, supposedly working on a color scheme, her mind a blank. The only colors she was able to summon to mind were the myriad blues of Drew's eyes. She'd get up and walk around her office, trying to summon visual images of the rooms, their occupants, the way the sun shone in the windows at various times of the day. She did hatha-yoga exercises, hoping for a measure of serenity, but her mind would not be freed of Drew and Selby.

"I don't know what's wrong," she told Rita one day when things weren't going right. She felt sluggish, apathetic.

"Maybe you need a vacation," suggested Rita.

Maybe I need Drew, Cathryn said to herself in desperation, and she called him for the first time in a week. He didn't answer his phone, however, and she hung up feeling lost and alone. He'd always been there when she needed him before. Before Selby came.

HE SHOWED UP at her apartment one night later that week. It was a telling comment on their relationship that he didn't appear at her door unannounced as he usually did, but had Gurney call ahead on the intercom.

He couldn't, Drew thought, turn up at her door sure of his welcome. He wasn't sure of anything anymore, much less that she'd want to see him on the spur of the moment, the way she had before. Everything, it seemed to him, had changed.

She opened the door, and he thought he saw a gladness in her remarkable eyes. Then a mask of self-control slipped over her features, banishing spontaneity and replacing the Cathryn he loved with a stranger he barely knew.

He gathered her into his arms, feeling how stiff she was. He winced inwardly at the knowledge of what her inflexibility meant. It was over for them; he had known this rigidity, this withholding of a self before, with Talma. But he couldn't just walk out the door. There were things that had to be said.

"We need to talk," he said heavily.

"Come in and sit down," she said, dreading this. Just looking at his face, so golden from the sun, his blue eyes blazing into her with that uncanny perception of what she was feeling and thinking, made her dread their conversation even more.

They sat on the couch in front of the long windows, the blue ocean and sky beyond. She had never looked lovelier to him than she did at this moment, he thought, despite the unhappiness evident between them.

"Cathryn, I've been thinking about marriage, and I want you to know that it's still what I want, more than anything else in the world." He suddenly reconsidered; perhaps he shouldn't have started out that way. Maybe it would have been better to begin with preliminaries.

She was utterly bewildered by her contradictory feelings. If she loved him, she'd want to marry him, wouldn't she? In spite of everything?

"I love you, Drew," she said, her voice sounding to her as though it came from a long way away. "I love you, but I can't marry you."

"Is it Selby?" he asked, his curt tone belying his desperation.

She closed her eyes, then opened them. She stood up and walked to the wide window, looking out at the ocean. The ocean was rough this evening, huge breakers hurling themselves onto the shore. Some fool was windsurfing down the beach, sailing alone on a fragile craft, weaving his way through the treacherous

Interior Designs

breakers. Then, as she watched, he capsized in the wash of a too-high wave. She felt like that windsurfer; she'd been sailing along on what seemed like a worthy craft, but had been washed out by something that was, in the end, too big to handle.

She turned to face Drew. "It isn't Selby. I love her; you know that. No, it isn't Selby. It's me. Being involved intimately with two other people takes time. I can't see giving up any part of my work or my career, the things that make me what I am. It's not just earning money, it's the part of me that I would be losing if I didn't do all that I'm capable of accomplishing."

There was no doubting the sincerity with which she spoke, but it seemed to him that she was leaving something out.

He went to stand beside her, taking care not to touch her. "You wouldn't have to give up your work. Just slow down a bit to make time for other things. And aren't you forgetting something? You've learned what you can be through your work. A thoroughly professional interior designer, a successful one. You design interiors for everyone else, Cathryn, but your own interior is empty. Give yourself space to grow, to be something that you haven't ever been."

"You mean as Selby's stepmother?" The amber in her eyes blazed "Caution."

He nodded, watching her intently. "And as my wife," he said.

Cathryn's shoulders slumped. "I've never fancied myself a mother type," she said quietly. "You know that."

"You're wonderful with Selby," he told her gently.

He wanted commitment, she realized, and nothing less. And she couldn't give it. With this man, she had wanted the communion of their bodies and the touching of their souls. She'd wanted more than she was willing to give.

She didn't have to tell him. He knew. Slowing down wasn't in her repertoire; she was caught up in her success and the perpetuation of it. She wasn't ready to commit herself to him or to Selby, and perhaps she never would be.

He knew that he could play on her sympathies and get certain immediate results. He knew that he could plead with her, toss in a few remarks about how difficult it was to be a single father, and she would probably give in a little, albeit reluctantly. He could impress his need on her, convince her that she was the one he wanted to help him survive his problems.

But those would be cheap shots. In depending on those arguments, he would be settling for less than either he or Cathryn deserved. He wanted her. But he wanted nothing less than total commitment on her part, the kind of commitment that he was willing to give to her. Anything else would diminish the love they had for each other.

When she didn't speak, he said gently, "I'll go," and turned toward the door. She was painfully conscious that he expected more of her.

"Drew?" Her voice was urgent, and for one heart-stopping moment, he thought she might be going to tell him what he wanted to hear more than anything in the world.

"I wish it didn't have to be this way," she said. Even as she spoke, the desire to be held in his arms again flooded through her.

"It doesn't," he said. Her eyes upon him were a cool green. He'd forgotten how indomitable she could be.

"We can see each other occasionally," she offered, knowing it wasn't enough.

"Shall I call you?"

"If you like," she said, without much hope. She felt sick and shaken in the aftermath of her tumbling emotions.

No spark of happiness lighted his features. With a twisting, wrenching pain she watched him walk away from her, out of her life.

Chapter Thirteen

"WE JUST GOT MARRIED!"

It was Susannah calling long-distance, waking Cathryn from a sound sleep.

"Who got married?"

"We did—Avery and me. We eloped to San Francisco!"

"That's wonderful, Susannah. Are you aware that it's three-thirty in the morning?" Cathryn was groggy and confused. But wasn't it just like Susannah to forget about the time difference and to call in the middle of the night?

"Well, I wanted you to be the first to know. You and Judy, of course."

"And what did Judy say?" Cathryn reached over and switched on her bedside light. Slowly, slowly, she was waking up. Susannah was married again! Why should Cathryn feel surprised?

"Oh, I called you first. I'll give Judy a ring when we hang up."

"I'll call Judy in the morning and tell her the good news," said Cathryn hastily. "No need to disturb her whole family at this hour."

"Maybe not. You don't sound impressed, Cathryn. I thought you'd be happy for me."

"I am. Oh, I am, Susannah. I hope you'll be very happy." She said this as sincerely as she could, knowing full well that, with Susannah, this marriage had every chance of bombing out like all her previous ones.

"So when are you coming to see us in Connecticut? You said you'd redecorate the house. Will you?"

"Well, I—"

"Come on, Cathryn. You *did* say you would. And I want you to meet Avery. He's eager to meet you. How soon can you get there?"

"To Connecticut? Susannah, do you have any idea what it's like for a working woman? I have schedules, meetings, a conference." Cathryn stopped and thought. The League of Interior Designer's conference, where she was going to speak, was happening in New York. It was an easy commute from the city to Greenwich, Connecticut, where Avery—and now Susannah—lived, she knew; Avery worked in New York City.

"You know," Cathryn said, warming to the idea, "I'll be attending a conference in New York the first week in October. I could fly up a few days early, perhaps."

Susannah squealed. "Could you? Oh, Cathryn, how wonderful! Please do." She lowered her voice. "I know I can't stand living in that awful house any longer than I have to. Avery's given me carte blanche. He says I can fix it up any way I like. Oh, I can't wait to see you!"

Cathryn smiled at Susannah's enthusiasm. "I'll check out the possibilities and let you know if I can make it. In the meantime, aren't you supposed to be on your honeymoon?"

"Yes," and Susannah giggled. "Avery bought me a black chiffon negligee with ostrich feathers. You should see it on me. I look like a *Playboy* centerfold."

Cathryn laughed. "In that case, Avery and not I should see it. Hang up, Susannah."

"Good idea. Let me know when you're arriving, will you?"

"If I'm arriving," corrected Cathryn.

"When," insisted Susannah.

"All right, when," Cathryn said, sighing.

Oh, well, why not? thought Cathryn as she replaced the receiver. It would be fun to see Susannah, and design an interior to suit her irrepressible personality. She hadn't had any fun lately, now that Drew was out of her life. And it would be good to feel the comfort Susannah could give her at this difficult time in her life. Susannah, at least, would be less judgmental than Judy, if only because Susannah had experienced plenty of man problems of her own.

After Susannah's phone call, Cathryn didn't fall asleep again. Distractedly, she contrasted Susannah's happiness with her own misery: Susannah, who had made the commitment to marriage four times—and

Cathryn, who had never even seen her way clear to make that same commitment once. A sudden worry surfaced in Cathryn: Would seeing Susannah really be a comfort, or would it just remind of the risks she hadn't taken?

NEW YORK CITY evoked glamour and excitement for Cathryn. The people scurried through the airport, each person intent on his own life, his own business. The very air crackled with a sense of mission and purpose. It was so different from the unhurried atmosphere of Palm Beach at this time of year, when the town was just beginning to stir in preparation for the winter season.

The gleaming black limousine Susannah had sent for Cathryn was impressive, to say the least. The chauffeur accomplished the twenty-eight-mile drive to Greenwich in short order, and even after the sumptuous oceanfront mansions of Palm Beach, Avery Clark's estate on the outskirts of Greenwich made Cathryn gape. The curving drive wound through acres of woods before ending in front of an immense stone facsimile of a Norman castle.

"Cathryn!" It was Susannah, running across what was, so help her, a drawbridge. Susannah looked radiant.

They kissed the air beside each other's cheeks. Cathryn stared unabashedly up at the crenellated tower above them.

"I see what you mean about this house," said Cathryn with a grin.

"Yeah," replied Susannah ruefully. "Come on in—I've installed you in the southeast-tower guest room."

"The southeast *tower?*"

"Sure. Whoever built this place must've been an admirer of William the Conqueror. Isn't it awful?"

"Unusual," hedged Cathryn. "Whatever persuaded Avery to buy it?"

"His ex-wife, Queen Shirley."

"You call her Queen Shirley?"

"Well, only to Avery. And now you."

Arm in arm, they trooped across the drawbridge past a banded oaken door heavily encrusted with iron bolts. A suit of armor loomed up at them in the large dark-paneled hall. Susannah contemptuously smacked it on the knee. The resulting clang resounded from the high ceilings.

Susannah had not exaggerated the depressing decor: unrelentingly Jacobean furniture, black with age; ratty red-velvet draperies tasseled with gold fringe; dingy rugs, ugly paintings. And yet the place had possibilities: The study abounded with tall, mullioned windows, and the family room built across the back of the first floor overlooked a picturesque free-form swimming pool.

"This place will be fun to work with," declared Cathryn after a tour of the rest of the house. She and Susannah stood in the tower bedroom that was to be Cathryn's for the duration of her visit.

"I'm glad you think so," replied Susannah fervently. "And now, if you don't mind, I'll go see what the cook is doing to the roast. I tried to explain the recipe, but I just hired her last week and she barely speaks English. Dinner's at eight, so why don't you come down whenever you're ready? Avery will be home soon and he's dying to meet you."

Twilight had dusted the woods with silver light by the time Cathryn descended the winding tower staircase. From the family room—the only room which Susannah could bear to remain in for any length of time—Cathryn heard the murmur of voices and the bright tinkle of Susannah's laughter. Cathryn smiled upon hearing it. She didn't recall ever seeing Susannah this happy, not with husbands number one, two or three.

Susannah glided forward to greet her, her flowing crimson dress echoing the glowing embers in the fireplace beyond. Cathryn recognized Avery by the distinctive silver wings at his temples; suave, sophisticated and elegantly attired, he was everything Susannah had claimed.

"I'm delighted to meet you," Cathryn said, offering Avery her hand.

"Welcome," he said, smiling down at her. He pulled Susannah close to him. "Susannah and I want you to stay as long as you like. Don't be in a hurry to get back to Palm Beach. Susannah will enjoy having company here in this big place." He smiled fondly at his wife.

"I can't stay as long as I'd really like to because of my studio," began Cathryn, and before she knew it she was embarked on the stock explanation of her busy life, telling Avery about the speech she was going to make at the conference of interior designers and outlining her plans for the rest of the year.

Through it all, Avery listened carefully, thoughtfully, and Cathryn couldn't help but admire Susannah's current choice of husband. Avery, so interested and attentive, was the dignified counterpoint to Susannah's brashness. Perhaps this marriage would not go the way of Susannah's first three after all, thought Cathryn hopefully and with considerable surprise.

It was evident throughout dinner that Avery adored his wife. Communication between them was special and deep; they were entirely in tune with each other. *Just as Drew and I once were,* Cathryn thought unhappily. Why, oh, why, when she saw another couple happy together, did her mind always fly to thoughts of how it might have been if she and Drew...But why think of it? What was the use?

She pushed the thought of Drew from her mind. In spite of her sadness, which contrasted with Susannah and Avery's happiness, Cathryn turned her attention at once to the job she had traveled here to do.

She spent the next few days studying the house, talking with Avery and Susannah to determine their preferences in home decor, and studying how they spent their days.

"Mostly, I want this house to be comfortable," insisted Susannah, flipping through color charts. "And colorful. Welcoming, so that people will want to come and visit."

As she listened, Cathryn formulated a design plan in her head, one that included taking advantage of the lovely big family room overlooking the pool, making it the heart of the house. Since Avery had assured her that money was no object, she would also order new furniture for the entire downstairs, perhaps including lots of European antiques, preferably in light woods. She made quick preliminary sketches of drapery treatments that would take advantage of the quaint mullioned windows. Susannah and Avery were thrilled when she described how their house would come alive with its new look.

"You know, this estate is charming, Susannah," Cathryn told her friend earnestly a day or two before she was planning to leave. "That is, once you get over the shock of the castle. But the trees, this winding road—all of it is beautiful."

They were walking along the driveway beneath foliage bright with autumn colors. Their path was strewn with leaves of brown, ocher and russet. Shafts of light from the autumn sun shone through treetops, casting patterns on the stone walls of the castle and mellowing them into a charming backdrop. As Cathryn spoke, a saffron-colored leaf floated down and landed on Susannah's powder-blue cashmere sweater; impatiently she flicked it away. The air blew cool with the breath of approaching winter.

"I like this place, too," Susannah said, smiling. "The country, the fresh air—well, it's not Palm Beach. I'll miss the sunshine this winter. But I'm happy here."

"You *are* happy, aren't you?" asked Cathryn curiously.

"Oh, very. I've never been so happy in my life. I love Avery so much."

"And he loves you. It's easy to see that."

Susannah turned serious eyes upon Cathryn. "It's the kind of love I hoped you would find with a man. Avery and I truly care about each other, Cathryn. I thought that with Drew you might—"

"No!" cried Cathryn sharply. It hurt even to hear Susannah speak his name.

They walked on in silence, Susannah biting her lip. "I'm sorry," she said quietly after a time. "I had no idea Drew was such a sensitive topic, even though you haven't mentioned him since you've been here."

"Forgive me for being so morose these days," said Cathryn unhappily. "I'm afraid I haven't been especially good company."

"Of course you have! But I admit that you haven't seemed quite your old self. Do you want to talk about it?"

Cathryn took her time in replying. "I got out of the relationship with Drew," she said finally. "It...it wasn't working out. He wanted to get married, and I couldn't."

"You couldn't? Why on earth not?" Susannah stared at her as though she had taken leave of her senses.

"My work, Susannah. I didn't have time for Drew and my work, especially after his daughter came. My work suffered, so..." She lifted her shoulders and let them drop. "He wanted to get married, but I couldn't see myself planning my life around the needs of a child, and—"

"You thought he wanted to marry you just so you'd take care of his little girl?" Susannah was incredulous.

"No, it wasn't like that. But Selby is part of him and would be very much a part of our marriage, especially if Drew gains custody of her, as he would like to. She's only seven, and she needs a lot of attention."

"I can sympathize," said Susannah. "After all, I got stuck with husband number two's Heather Marie. She used to bite me when he wasn't looking."

"Selby wasn't like that. She's a sweet child, very loving and dear and—"

"Then I don't understand the problem. If you love him and you like Selby—"

"I grew to love Selby," said Cathryn unhappily, fighting tears.

"Then you should have made room in your life for her," insisted Susannah resolutely. "Why couldn't you leave the nuts and bolts of Cathryn Mulqueen Interiors to your assistants? You've built it up, made it grow. Can't your business thrive on its own now, with just an occasional nod from you?"

"That's not the point. I *am* my work. I wouldn't be the same person without it. Don't you see?"

Susannah shook her head. "Not really. I don't think I'd let anything come between me and the man I love."

Living with Susannah and Avery, Cathryn had to admit that she'd been envious. The secret glances they shared, the quiet laughter when they thought they were alone, the tender touch when they believed she wasn't looking—all this had convinced her that Susannah and Avery were meant for each other and were deeply in love.

"You and I are not much alike, Susannah," was all Cathryn said.

Before the silence became brooding, Susannah suggested they turn back toward the house. Suddenly she said, "Avery has tickets for a dance next week. It's a charity ball in the Grand Ballroom of the Waldorf-Astoria Hotel, and we'd like you to go with us. You will, won't you?"

"But I—"

"Of course you will. It'll give you something to look forward to after that stuffy conference. And it'll get your mind off Drew."

"I don't know what I'd wear, and—"

"You can wear anything and look like a princess. Oh, please go, Cathryn. It would be such a good time, honestly."

"But I won't know anyone, so—"

"I've already lined up a date for you."

"A date!"

"Yes," Susannah said, giggling. "So you can hardly say no, because that would put me in the position of telling him you canceled, and I've already given you a big buildup!"

Thoroughly exasperated, Cathryn said, "You had no right to ask someone without my permission! For heaven's sake, Susannah, will you ever grow up?"

"Probably not." Susannah laughed, and she looked so delighted with herself that Cathryn found herself acquiescing.

"All right," she said, shaking her head. "But don't ever put me in this position again, you idjit."

Susannah smiled. "Don't be silly. Would I take my chances again?"

Probably, thought Cathryn, but she couldn't be truly angry. Susannah, in her own way, was only trying to cheer her up.

CONTACT WITH OTHER INTERIOR DESIGNERS from all over the country stimulated her, and there was so much happening at the conference that Cathryn had little time to dwell on her own thoughts. That was good. She didn't want to dwell on them, didn't want to think about Drew and Selby.

But there were those inevitable moments alone in her hotel suite when she had all too much time to ruminate about past events. At those times she resolutely chided herself. The affair with Drew was *over.* It was over because she had wanted it to be.

Even after all these weeks, she missed his bright presence in her life, his openness and honesty, his capacity for tenderness, his total understanding. Being around Susannah and Avery had only made her remember painfully how rewarding a close relationship with a man could be.

Missing Selby was almost as bad as missing Drew. She knew now that she should never have allowed her natural liking for the child to intensify into love. It was a lesson she thought she had learned with Terry Ballard and his adorable little boys. But, no, she had allowed herself to be drawn willingly into Drew and Selby's family unit and had experienced a new kind of encompassing love that included all three of them. Now that it was gone, there was a hole in her life. It made the parting from Drew all the more wrenching.

Her week in New York would help. Here she was caught up in activities that would culminate at the banquet at which she was to speak.

The matronly president of the League of Interior Designers took Cathryn under her wing. The morning of the banquet she asked a surprised Cathryn, "How would you like to be on television? They want somebody to appear on one of the local cable network shows on Friday morning to talk about the League. Will you do it, Cathryn? You're such a good spokesperson for our organization, and you're so photogenic!"

"Of course," said Cathryn. "But what will the interview be about?"

"Your life, your career, current design trends. You know."

That night after the banquet Cathryn took a quick shower and slipped on her terry-cloth robe before she sat down at the desk in her hotel suite with pages from the speech she had just given, hoping to capture a few of the highlights. This would help her to think clearly when she was being interviewed on television the next morning, she reasoned.

She jotted a few sentences on paper, and then restlessly tossed the paper into the wastebasket. She stood up and walked the length of the hotel room. She plunged her hands into the robe's deep pockets, and her fingers closed over something hard and round. It was the shell she had found on the beach at Hobe Sound months ago when she had confided in Drew her fears about sharing him.

She stared at the seashell, remembering how she had studied it that day, thinking about the inner design of it.

The intricate interior of Cathryn Mulqueen had protected her from everything until Drew Sedgwick came along to tear down all the barriers, to change the very form of her beliefs, to let in space and light where none had been able to penetrate the convoluted passages before.

And with Drew she had discovered that she no longer needed the protection of the barriers she had erected to keep out love and caring. She had learned to love and to share. Learning the art of loving and sharing was every bit as important as learning to build a career, and in fact, it held the promise of becoming even more fulfilling.

She whirled toward the desk, and the sudden stirring of air ruffled the papers on which her speech was written. They flew onto the floor, where they lay like so many leaves scattered by the wind. And all at once, Cathryn was haunted by certain inescapable thoughts that she had been avoiding for much too long.

She had sacrificed to get to the top of her field because her work gave her pleasure and a sense of reward. And now, thinking back on the past few weeks when she had struggled with thoughts of Drew, finding it difficult to concentrate on anything she was doing—the new office building in West Palm Beach, even Susannah's castle—she had to admit that her work was no longer pleasant for her, not as fulfilling. In fact, it had become a tremendous burden.

It was an earthshaking realization. The new office building awaited her attention back in Palm Beach, and the idea of returning to it was suddenly loathsome. She dreaded sitting down at her desk; despite her protestations to Susannah, she would rather do anything than get back to work! Such protestations were nothing more than the force of habit.

She sat in her hotel suite and stared at the wall, utterly shattered. Because if her work was her whole life, and if her work was no longer meaningful, then her life had no meaning.

She stood up and paced the floor, driven into motion by the torment of her thoughts. Her first reaction was stubborn denial. No, it couldn't be! Hadn't she always said that her work gave definition to her personality, that she wouldn't be the person she was without it? Suddenly she had come face-to-face with the person she was, and she didn't like that person— that lonely, ever-remote person—very much. She had never perceived herself with such clarity before. Was this the way Drew had seen her? If so, what had given

him the strength, the caring, the steadfast and endur-
ing persistence to, as he had put it, melt the ice?"

Only one thing, she realized out of the depths of her
solemn soul searching, only one thing could have given
him that persistence: love.

She spent a sleepless night. The next morning, after
carefully applying makeup to conceal the violet shadows smudged beneath her eyes, she approached the
television interview with trepidation but with a single-
mindedness and determination that surprised her. She
would do the show, she would get it over with. And
then she would fly back to Palm Beach and make definite plans to diminish her involvement with Cathryn
Mulqueen Interiors.

How would she accomplish it? Plans reeled through
her head, one after the other. Let Zohra and Renee
manage the business? Call the pesky lawyer for Designers International and tell him she was ready to sell
Cathryn Mulqueen Interiors? Take the money and go
on a long trip, a vacation during which she'd ponder
the direction of her future? Maybe she'd even find
time to begin painting again.

It was too late to do anything about what had happened with Drew; he was out of her life. It wasn't too
late, however, to arrange her life differently. To work
on her own interior, to let in space and light, to design it so that there would be time for important
things, now that she knew what the important things
were. It was not having the important things that made
it clear to her at last that Judy and Ron and Susannah, and especially Drew, had been right all along.

She must get through the television interview that she had promised to do, and, of course, she must attend the ball tomorrow night. Those were her immediate obligations, and she'd always been one to honor obligations. But then she'd take time off to think about her own interior designs.

Chapter Fourteen

He shouldn't have crashed this party, thought Drew, watching them. He might have known she'd have someone else. He didn't know who it was, but he was a handsome man, and he was gazing down at Cathryn with unabashed desire. Well, what man wouldn't? Cathryn was beautiful, sexy and as desirable as any woman he'd ever seen. The guy would be crazy not to want her.

He'd spent the morning rounding up evening clothes that fit him. Drew knew after watching that segment on the cable network that he had to see her, if only from a distance.

The woman interviewer had introduced the piece in a way that had made him interrupt his shaving routine and rush out of the bathroom to turn up the volume. The introduction had mentioned the League of Interior Designers' conference, a conference Drew had known nothing about until then.

And then, there was his Cathryn, cool and composed as usual, smiling graciously and answering questions, playing to the camera in all the right places, yet somehow remaining distant and one step removed. She talked about her work, about her life, and she seemed to be the epitome of success. She was so beautiful that it wrung his heart, left it empty: her hair, her hands clasped in her lap, the way she enunciated her words. He loved her; he had tried to get over her when he'd realized that he couldn't have her, but he loved her still.

It had taken more than one phone call to Judy before he found out how to reach Cathryn. Even then, all that Judy would do was to give him Susannah's new phone number in Connecticut.

But when Susannah heard his voice, she went suddenly silent. And then she told him exactly where Cathryn could be found that evening.

And so here he stood at the edge of the dance floor in the Grand Ballroom of the Waldorf-Astoria Hotel, watching the love of his life gazing raptly into the eyes of another man.

CATHRYN HAD PREPARED for the ball at the Waldorf-Astoria without enthusiasm. Such events were superfluous, but she had promised Susannah, and Susannah had gone to the trouble of supplying an escort.

Cathryn had piled her hair on top of her head in a loose knot, allowing one silken strand to curl in a ringlet down one side. She wore a simple gown of rich jade-green, its V neck plunging and skirt slit to the knee. In her ears she wore a pair of dazzling diamond-drop earrings. Even to herself she looked stunning and worthy of any date Susannah produced.

When Susannah and party arrived at her hotel suite, Cathryn was ready. After the knock sounded on the door of her room, Susannah called out, "It's just us, Cathryn," and Cathryn released the chain and opened the door. Susannah, radiant in rose-red silk, was flanked by two men, one of them Avery, and another who looked vaguely familiar.

"Cathryn," said Susannah breathlessly, turning to the stunning man on her right, "this is Will Atherton. You remember. My first husband."

Cathryn did remember. Except for Avery, he had been the best-looking of Susannah's husbands. Cathryn recalled being a bridesmaid at their wedding, and how, at the time, she had joined Judy and the other bridesmaids in gushing over the bridegroom's handsome looks. He was tall, smiling, affable and supremely sexy, with a rakish mustache and a diabolical gleam in his eye.

"Nice to see you again," she said politely, wondering how in the world Susannah had happened to contrive a date for Cathryn with her first husband.

Susannah read her friend's mind. "It's all right," she said hastily with a confirming look from Avery. "Will and I are still good friends."

"Oh," said Cathryn doubtfully, wondering how she was going to make it through the evening. The arrangement struck her as, well, *odd*.

"Do you have a drink around here anywhere?" Will wanted to know. His eyes swept the room, presumably looking for a liquor bottle.

"Uh, no, but we could call room service."

"I've always got my flask," said Will, and with a grin he flashed a silver bottle out of an inside coat pocket and upended it. Cathryn caught the unmistakable odor of gin.

Cathryn wanted to laugh at the distasteful expression on Avery's face. Clearly he had not known this side of his wife's ex-husband.

"Shall we go?" said Avery quickly, offering Susannah his arm.

Reluctantly, Cathryn replaced her hand through the crook of Will's elbow, trying to keep a straight face. At this rate, Susannah's husband number one would be tipsy by ten o'clock. Which was just as well, because then she'd be able to duck out.

They proceeded by taxi to the Grand Ballroom of the Waldorf-Astoria. When they stepped out of the elevator on the floor where the ballroom was located, they met teeming groups of men and women dressed to the hilt in long formal dresses and white-tie-and-tails for the occasion. The sweet strains of violins floated over the milling gathering, and the lobby of the ballroom was bright and well-lighted.

"What are you *doing*?" she hissed to Susannah when Avery was out of hearing range at the coat checkroom. "How on earth did you happen to set me up with *him*?" Will lingered behind a potted plant, surreptitiously fumbling with his flask.

For once, Susannah looked distressed. "Will called up to wish me a happy marriage, and I asked him to escort you to the ball. Avery had met him once before and liked him, and I thought it seemed like a good idea at the time. I had no idea Will was drinking so much." She shrugged helplessly and surveyed the crowd uneasily as if she were looking for someone.

"Well, if I disappear halfway through this, please understand. I have no desire to spend the whole evening holding up a man who is so drunk he can't walk, much less dance."

"Cathryn, I'm sorry, really I am. If he gets to be too much of a nuisance, we can send him home. For that matter, I suppose we could leave now if we think of some excuse." But for some reason, Susannah looked reluctant.

"No, no, I can manage," Cathryn replied hastily as Avery caught up with them and Will slipped out from behind the plant.

"Now," said Will, smiling his charismatic smile, "how about dancing with me, Cathryn? As I recall, we danced rather well together at my wedding reception."

Will took hold of her arm, guiding her firmly toward the highly polished ballroom dance floor. At least he seemed to know where he was going. With one last nervous look back at Susannah and Avery, Cathryn allowed herself to be propelled.

As they reached the dance floor, the band quickly ended its piece and, with a great deal of fanfare, began a new one, a waltz. Will pulled her into his arms and focused dreamy eyes on Cathryn. She was the only one close enough to notice how bleary they were.

Will's mustache twitched as they rounded the floor for the third time. "I could use another drink right about now, how about you?"

"No thanks," she said, concentrating on her dancing. He was a good dancer, at least, if a trifle loose. He flung them in extravagant swoops around the ballroom.

"Do you have a boyfriend back home? Anybody special?"

"No." She hoped her tone of voice would convince him that this wasn't an avenue of conversation that she cared to pursue.

"Good. I've always liked you, Cathryn. You know that, don't you?" He pulled her a bit closer; she edged away again.

"Mm," she said noncommittally, concentrating on following him.

The waltz ended and everyone clapped. The band struck up another waltz.

"Hey, let's not sit down! Let's dance this one, too!" Will Atheron smiled at her and suppressed a belch. She didn't resist when he drew her into his arms again; there was no point in making a scene. They waltzed in great swirling circles around the dance floor. The throng of people on the sidelines blurred into a sea of faces.

A spotlight switched on, beaming down at them from one of the balconies. Somebody with a camera was busily filming the scene on the dance floor.

She drew a deep breath, ignoring the smell of gin. It looked as though it was going to be a long night. If only someone would turn off that awful blinding spotlight!

ONCE THEY DIPPED SO CLOSE to him that Drew thought she must surely see him, but she was so wrapped up in Will Atherton that she stared right past.

How was he to get what he wanted—a chance to speak with her alone? There were so many people. In vain he tried to spot Susannah, who had assured him that she and her new husband would be there. They were nowhere in sight.

What should he do? He had to talk with Cathryn. It was the only reason he had come there tonight. He racked his brain, trying to think. He hadn't come this far only to give up. But it was so hard to think of anything when she was in the arms of someone else.

In sheer desperation, it occurred to Drew that perhaps it would not be improper etiquette for him to cut in. Of course. It was the only logical course of action.

He should have thought of it in the beginning.

Cathryn couldn't believe her eyes. Her vision was hazy from dizziness, to be sure, and the spotlight made her see dots. But she could have sworn that she had spied Drew Sedgwick standing at the edge of the dance floor as she and Will whirled around the ballroom.

She looked for him again as they approached the place where he had been. Suddenly her palm went damp in Will's hand. It was either Drew Sedgwick or his exact double, all dressed up in white-tie-and-tails.

She and Will glided away, and she snapped her head around to stare. Her eyes locked with his, and there was no doubt in her mind that it was Drew.

But how...? Why?

What on earth would Drew Sedgwick be doing here at the Waldorf at the exact same time she was?

But perhaps she had been wrong. The next time they swooped past the place where Drew had been standing, he wasn't there.

She bit her lip and fought back tears, and she stared resolutely at the space over Will Atherton's right shoulder.

Obviously, it had been a mirage. She had thought about Drew Sedgwick so much in the past few weeks that she was imagining him in places where he couldn't possibly be. It was just one more sign that she needed a vacation, and the sooner, the better.

"May I cut in?"

Cathryn's heart fell to the pit of her stomach. Will looked dazed. They both stopped dancing and stared at Drew Sedgwick.

"Do you know this guy?" Will asked Cathryn with a frown.

"I, well, yes. We're old friends." Try as she might, she could not take her eyes off Drew's face. His blue eyes searched hers. He couldn't be real, he couldn't! But did a mirage walk and talk? Did it clasp your hand?

"I have to see somebody about something anyway," said Will ungraciously. He wove around through the other dancers, barely avoiding collision.

"Let's get out of here," said Drew. He held on to her hand tightly, as though she would disappear if he let go.

"But Will is my date. Susannah..." Her eyes scanned the crowd, looking for her friend.

"I've squared it with Susannah. You have her blessing. Avery's going to put Will in a cab and send him home." Drew charged into the crowd around the dance floor, pulling her with him. Where the crowd thinned out in the back of the room, he paused and put his arm around Cathryn's waist.

"Drew?"

"I have to talk to you," he said firmly. A glance toward the lobby of the ballroom told him that people were still arriving. The elevators would be mobbed, and they would be much too slow.

"Is there a quick way out of here?" he muttered in desperation.

"There's bound to be a service elevator near the kitchen," she said. "But why do we have to hurry?"

"We have a lot of time to make up," he said, urging her toward the swinging doors where the waiters kept going in and out. On the other side of the doors was an elevator, a big one. Drew pushed her inside and punched a button on the panel. The door closed after them and the elevator sped downward. Cathryn was afraid to look at him for fear she'd laugh. This was ridiculous!

They reached the basement with a solid *clunk*, and the elevator door opened automatically to reveal a long concrete corridor that veered off into labyrin-thine passages beneath the hotel.

"Now what?" asked Cathryn, who had made up her mind not to be surprised at anything in this crazy sequence of events.

Drew, just guessing at their whereabouts, pulled Cathryn toward a flight of stairs topped by a door that proved to open on an alley furnished with several overturned garbage cans and a heap of black plastic bags bursting with trash.

"Where are we going?" she asked him as they stood indecisively in the alley.

"We're not staying in this alley, I can tell you that," Drew said, rushing toward the street and pulling her along in his wake. They reached the street and, al-most as though it was written into the script, a cab pulled over to the curb.

Drew pushed her, none too gently, inside.

"Where to?" said the cabdriver, running his eyes over them curiously. They didn't look like the type of people to come running out of an alley in New York.

For the first time, Drew drew a blank. "Where to?" he said to Cathryn.

She stifled a smile, but she was equal to the occa-sion. "Central Park. The horse-drawn carriages."

"Good idea," said Drew approvingly. He slipped his arm around the back of the seat and toyed with the strand of hair that curled along one side of her neck. She'd left her evening cape behind, but she scarcely noticed the autumn chill in the air.

"Nice to see you again," Drew said, an understatement.

"Why are you here?" she asked him. His eyes were bright cerulean-blue above his wide smile.

"I'm trying to get you back," he answered truthfully. She looked confused. "I saw you being interviewed on the cable network this morning. That's how I knew you were in New York. It was a terrific interview, by the way."

"It was just an ordinary interview." She shrugged.

"But you're not an ordinary person. You looked gorgeous," he told her.

"Oh," she said. Now that the initial shock had worn off, she still found it hard to believe that Drew Sedgwick could be in New York now, at the same time she was. The odds seemed stacked too heavily against such a situation.

The cab stopped. "Central Park," said the driver.

Drew pressed bills into the man's hand. They got out of the taxi and into one of the horse-drawn carriages.

"Drive slowly," Drew told the driver, who tipped his hat genially. Drew slid close to Cathryn so that they sat with their thighs touching.

"What are you doing in New York?" asked Cathryn, unable to contain her curiosity any longer.

"Conferring with Talma's lawyers," he said, surprising her.

"What about?"

"Child custody." His eyes rested warmly on her face, taking her all in. There was no icy distance between them now, and he was glad.

"Has something happened?"

"Talma wants to stay in Italy with Alfredo, and she plans to take Selby out of the country. I've been looking into their life-style, and I'm totally against Selby's living with Talma. I've enrolled her in school in Palm Beach, and I've decided that I'm going to press for custody, even if Talma wants to fight it. These past months have shown me that Selby's stronger emotionally than I'd imagined, and she's sure that she wants to live with me."

"Oh, Drew." Cathryn was surprised at this, and yet not so surprised. And also disconcerting were the feelings of elation that were surfacing in her own mind.

"What do you think about it?" A lot hinged on her answer; Drew waited almost breathlessly. If she acted disappointed, he'd know it would never work out. Now that he was going to try to gain custody of his daughter, Cathryn would have to want Selby just as much as she wanted him. Because there was no doubt in his mind that Cathryn still loved him. It was written all over her face. Somehow, some way, if indeed she wanted Selby, they would work out a marriage. They had to. It was as simple as that.

"I think it's wonderful about Selby," she answered dispelling all his doubts. "Wonderful."

His eyes sought hers and found them. She touched his cheek gently. "I've made a mistake, Drew. A terrible mistake."

His arms went around her, drew her close, feeling her bones melt against his.

"Would you like to try again? Maybe try it until we get it right?"

"Our relationship, you mean?" Her head tilted back so that she could see his face. He was smiling at her more tenderly than she could have imagined.

"Yes, our relationship, and more when you're ready. I still want to marry you, Cathryn."

She placed her head on his shoulder, and it was a homecoming of sorts. "I have to finish my work on the office building. And I'm designing an interior for Susannah's house in Connecticut. But then..."

"Then what?"

"Then...I don't know. I'm not going to go on the way I have been. I'm either going to sell Cathryn Mulqueen Interiors or turn over more control to my assistants."

He rested his cheek against her forehead. They could hear the sound of the horse's hooves on the hard pavement. It was as though they were far away from the city and everything else. But he knew Cathryn, knew how she felt and thought about her career. "Are you sure that's what you want? Sure you can be happy not working twelve and fourteen hours a day?"

"I'm sure," she said convincingly. "Very, very sure."

"Selling seems like such a drastic measure. Maybe we could work out something with Sedgwick's. You know, expand your Design Boutique so that customers can only obtain your services through the store. You could let Zohra and Renee handle most of the business, let them actually run the show. But you could handle designing for certain clients, be very selective."

"I hadn't thought of that. It's a possibility, isn't it? Oh, Drew, I like the idea!" Her smile when she looked up at him was radiant, glowing.

"I'm going to fight for custody of Selby," he told her, "but I'm well aware that it may not work out. It's going to be a nasty battle. I wouldn't go through with if I didn't think I'd win. I'll need your support and help, and so will Selby. I may need your consolation if I lose. This won't be easy, Cathryn. It's going to be hanging over our heads for a long time."

"Everything may not be wonderful all the time," she said, slowly and earnestly. "Life isn't like that. But we'll have each other, and that's what is important to me."

"And what if I don't get custody of Selby? You won't be disappointed?"

She sat up straight and stared at him. "Of course I'll be disappointed! But it won't affect the way I feel about you. I'll stand by both you and Selby and help any way I can. If you don't get custody, Selby will still be able to visit us in the summers or whenever else we can arrange it. What's important is that we love each other."

"I'm going to stop spending as much time at work myself," he told her. "I've cut way back on my hours, but I'm going to cut back more. Bud Gurney is perfectly capable of taking over a lot of the business of running a chain of department stores. That way I'll have more time to spend with Selby. And with you."

He tightened his arms around her, feeling a transfiguring joy that eclipsed any emotion he'd ever felt. She reached up and stroked his hair gently once before curving her fingers around the nape of his neck, where they fit so well.

"I love you so much, Cathryn," he said unsteadily.

"Do you still want to marry me?" she asked, her cheek against his chest.

He looked down at her face, her dear and beautiful face. He pulled slightly away and fumbled in a pocket.

Cathryn's eyes widened at the sight of the large gleaming square-cut emerald encircled by a wreath of small brilliant diamonds. She held her breath as Drew slipped the ring on her left ring finger and kissed the skin above it.

"I told you once that you should wear emeralds," he said softly, his adoring eyes never leaving hers. "And as my wife, you will. Yes, my Cathryn, I do want to marry you. But what about you? Will you marry me?"

"Tomorrow, if you like," she said serenely, surely.

"Tomorrow? But there's the license to get, and Selby will want to be there, and—"

"Tomorrow or whenever," she amended, snuggling even closer. "And do you have any plans for tonight?"

He smiled at her tenderly, lovingly. "Tonight, tomorrow and always," he said, lowering his lips to hers.

Harlequin Intrigue

**Because
romance
can be quite
an adventure.**

WORLDWIDE LIBRARY IS YOUR TICKET TO ROMANCE, ADVENTURE AND EXCITEMENT

Experience it all in these big, bold Bestsellers— Yours exclusively from WORLDWIDE LIBRARY WHILE QUANTITIES LAST

To receive these Bestsellers, complete the order form, detach and send together with your check or money order (include 75¢ postage and handling), payable to WORLDWIDE LIBRARY, to:

In the U.S.
WORLDWIDE LIBRARY
Box 52040
Phoenix, AZ
85072-2040

In Canada
WORLDWIDE LIBRARY
P.O. Box 2800, 5170 Yonge Street
Postal Station A, Willowdale, Ontario
M2N 6J3

Quant.	Title	Price
_____	**WILD CONCERTO**, Anne Mather	$2.95
_____	**A VIOLATION**, Charlotte Lamb	$3.50
_____	**SECRETS**, Sheila Holland	$3.50
_____	**SWEET MEMORIES**, LaVyrle Spencer	$3.50
_____	**FLORA**, Anne Weale	$3.50
_____	**SUMMER'S AWAKENING**, Anne Weale	$3.50
_____	**FINGER PRINTS**, Barbara Delinsky	$3.50
_____	**DREAMWEAVER,** Felicia Gallant/Rebecca Flanders	$3.50
_____	**EYE OF THE STORM**, Maura Seger	$3.50
_____	**HIDDEN IN THE FLAME**, Anne Mather	$3.50
_____	**ECHO OF THUNDER**, Maura Seger	$3.95
_____	**DREAM OF DARKNESS**, Jocelyn Haley	$3.95

YOUR ORDER TOTAL	$_____
New York and Arizona residents add appropriate sales tax	$_____
Postage and Handling	$___.75
I enclose	$_____

NAME _____

ADDRESS _____ APT.# _____

CITY _____

STATE/PROV. _____ ZIP/POSTAL CODE _____
WW3

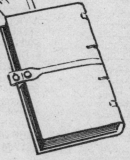